I0663977

The Unparalleled Adventure of One Hans Pfaall and Other Early Science Fiction Tales

www.firestonebooks.com

The Unparalleled Adventure of One Hans Pfaall and Other Early Science Fiction Tales

2012 Edition
Published by Firestone Books

The Comical History of the States and Empires of the Moon
and
Micromegas

Edited by David Lear

ISBN: 978-1-909608-08-5

Printed and bound by CreateSpace, USA

www.firestonebooks.com

Contents

Introduction

The earliest science fiction tales flickered into existence some two thousand years ago, with Greek and Roman works like Cicero's *Dream of Scipio*, and Lucian's *True History*. But such speculative tales were not to last – in Europe at least – and disappeared along with the Greek and Roman cultures that had borne them.

It was some fifteen hundred years before the genre re-emerged around the beginning of the sixteen hundreds, and a number of factors lay behind this apparent slumber and subsequent reawakening:

There was a decline in the amount of literature being written during the Dark Ages. (The term Dark Ages reflecting the relatively few works that were written in this period.) Then, in the Middle Ages, the idea of life on other planets was viewed as heresy in many quarters, and so it is likely that medieval writers judiciously avoided such subject matter.

In terms of the rebirth of science fiction, there were numerous factors, such as the declining power of the Church, and the advent of the printing press. There was also the circumnavigation of the Earth, causing the world, which once must have seemed to have endless oceans and unlimited possibilities, to suddenly appear a smaller and less interesting place. This meant writers of fantasy now had to look beneath the waves, underground, and out into space, for backdrops to their exotic tales.

The greatest influence on the pioneers of this genre however was the rise of modern science, where the mysteries of life and the universe were now explained by observation and reason, rather than by supernatural belief. Writers who wished to create believable fantasy could no longer employ magic in their tales, and instead turned to speculative technology – the basis of much science fiction to this day.

Editor's Note

With the advent of the printing press and the emergence of the novel, some four hundred years ago, authors were better able to weave long and intricate stories. This collection therefore contains not only short stories but excerpts from two early novels: *The Comical History of the States and Empires of the Moon* by Cyrano de Bergerac, and *The Blazing World* by Margaret Cavendish. We have decided to limit the number of novel excerpts to two, as we believe readers, as a general rule, would rather read short stories in their entirety than a series of excerpts. This does mean, however, that we have omitted a number of early science fiction works, such as Mary Shelley's *The Last Man*, an apocalyptic tale set in the year 2100, and also her most famous work, *Frankenstein*. We have also omitted Samuel Madden's *Memoirs of the Twentieth Century*, written in 1733, Sebastien Mercier's *The Year 2440*, written in 1770, and Jane C. Loudon's *The Mummy!* written in 1827, to name but a few.

In this collection we have the earliest tale of extraterrestrials from beyond our solar system (*Micromegas* by Voltaire), as well as an early apocalyptic tale (*The Conversation of Eiros and Charmion* by Edgar Allan Poe), and perhaps most interestingly of all, the idea of parallel worlds (*The Blazing World* by Margaret

Cavendish).

A lot of these early or proto-science fiction ideas may seem naive or quaint from today's perspective when we know, for instance, that there is no life on the Moon. But with a mixture of then-known science, some speculation, and not a little imagination, many of these tales would, at the time, have seemed quite plausible.

By this period, proto-science fiction authors are also clearly being influenced by other works within this genre (e.g. the influence of *Frankenstein* on Jane C. Loudon's *The Mummy!* or the influence of Poe's *The Unparalleled Adventure of One Hans Pfaall* on Verne's *From the Earth to the Moon*), so starting a clear lineage of science fiction stories that has carried on to this day.

Micromegas and the excerpt from *The Comical History of the States and Empires of the Moon* have both been newly translated for this collection, and all the tales in this volume have also been given their own brief introduction.

Comical History of the States and Empires of the Moon (excerpt)

Cyrano de Bergerac

Introduction

Hercule-Savinien de Cyrano de Bergerac (1619–1655) was a French writer, whose name is familiar today mainly because of the somewhat embellished biographical play *Cyrano de Bergerac* written by Edmond Rostand at the end of the nineteenth century.

The Comical History of the States and Empires of the Moon was written around 1648, but wasn't published until 1657, two years after Cyrano de Bergerac's death. It is, in part, a parody of Francis Godwin's *The Man in the Moone*. Like so much early science fiction the main character travels to the Moon and meets alien creatures, but with the main character using rockets to propel himself to this destination, we see a large technological leap to something more resembling 20th century space flight.

Edgar Allan Poe also refers to this work in his 1835 tale *The Unparalleled Adventure of One Hans Pfaall*, which itself influenced Jules Verne's science fiction classic *From the Earth to the Moon.*

Comical History of the States and Empires of the Moon

Cyrano de Bergerac

Chapter 1

How the Voyage was Conceived

One night, as I strolled home with two friends after attending a party, our conversation towards the Moon which was hanging, full and bright in the sky.

"I believe," said my first friend, "that the Moon is a window between Heaven and Earth."

"Pah!" said my second companion. "You ignorant man! What we see when we look up at the Moon, is merely the Sun spying on us through a hole in the heavens."

My friends argued in a good-natured manner about just what the Moon was, when at last they turned to me and begged my opinion.

"I think you're both utterly wrong," I said. "That brilliant object that we see at night and occasionally during the day, is a world just like ours, and just as they are a Moon to us, we are a Moon to them."

My friends burst with hearty laughter. "I think you should leave off the wine from now on," said one of my friends, and with that they laughed even more.

"A world like ours indeed!" mocked the other.

"I imagine," said I, raising my voice a little, "that there are beings on the Moon who would scoff at the idea that this world is inhabited. You might laugh, but there are many learned scholars who share my opinion."

But my words only caused my friends to laugh even more, so much so that they could barely walk, though I began to wonder if it wasn't they who had had too much to drink.

Outside my door I bade them goodnight, and watched them wander off in high-spirits.

Instead of making for bed, I went at once to my study. I didn't feel the least bit sleepy, and was curious to know more about the Moon.

I took out my key, but noticed the door was already ajar. I pushed the door open as quietly as possible, but the room was quite empty. I felt disconcerted, as I was the only person with a key to the study and I always left it locked.

More unusual than that, was a book by the philosopher Jerome Cardan lay open on my writing bureau. I had no particular desire to read the book, but just as I was about to close it and put it back on the shelf I suddenly stared at the page in front of me.

Here Cardan explained how two tall men had entered through a door that was locked, and spoken to him about a range of interesting topics. After a lengthy conversation, they eventually told him that they were inhabitants of the Moon. But before Cardan could ask any more, they disappeared.

I could not fathom how, after talking about life on the

Moon to two friends, this book should suddenly be lying on my desk on this very page.

"The Moon Men who appeared to Cardan," I whispered to myself, "They must have heard my conversation and come here. Is this an invitation, I wonder?" I put the book back on the shelf. "There's only one way I will ever know – I will have to journey to the Moon."

Chapter 2

The First Journey and the Unintended Destination

I meant every word about travelling to the Moon, and I moved to the country where I considered the possible ways of getting there. The method I finally chose involved wearing a great many bottles filled with dew, and standing outside on a hot summer's day.

As the sun heated the morning dew so taking it skywards, I hoped that I would be taken up as well. So I stood in a large empty field, looking quite a sight, and hoping that nobody would see me. Soon the bottles began to heat up and I felt my heels and then toes lifting off the ground. It was a strange sight watching the fields appear to shrink as I started to float upwards.

I passed through the clouds, but my flight did not take me towards the Moon. I waited for many hours hoping that that I might float in the right direction, but it seemed that I was simply treading air. In the end I gave up and decided to float back down into the field, so I smashed a few bottles, and began to descend.

I reckoned that given the time I set off, and given the length of my ascent, it must be around midnight. Once more I passed through the clouds, but when I landed it was still broad daylight.

This wasn't the only puzzle. I did not recognize my

surroundings at all. I saw, on the fringe of some woods, a cottage with a plume of smoke spiralling from the chimney. I tried to walk, and found myself bounding high into the air with each step, as though gravity barely recognized me. I smashed a few more bottles, and my strides resembled something of their previous length.

As I approached, I saw, between the trees, a number of dark people, all of whom were stark naked, but before I could call out to them, they disappeared. Perhaps they were startled by my dress or my floating movements – I couldn't say.

Before I reached the cottage, I saw two soldiers walking down a country lane, and I accosted them.

"Where am I?" I asked.

"You're in France," said one.

The other looked at me curiously. "Why on Earth are you dressed only in bottles? Are you on your way to see the Governor – to tell him the fleet has arrived?"

Hardly able to believe I was back in my country, I tried to explain my situation as best I could, but they didn't like my answers. Each of them grabbed one of my arms, and marched me to their leader.

The Governor, I soon found, was a kind and reasonable man. I told him of my adventure. He laughed, and told me I was in *New* France.

I recounted my flight, and then realised that though I had gone straight up then straight down, during the many hours I had spent in the sky, the Earth had revolved beneath me. That was how I'd ended up not in France, but in New France, Canada.

Chapter 3

Conversations about the Workings of the Universe

The Governor kindly let me stay in a bedroom in his own home, and as I readied myself for bed he knocked on my door.

"Come in," I called.

"I'm sorry to disturb you," he said.

"Not at all," I replied.

"I have just been debating your claims with some priests," said the Governor. "and they believe you are a sorcerer who has used magic to fly across the ocean. I, on the other hand, think there is a more rational explanation, though I must say I find it hard to believe that the Earth revolves. If that were really so, shouldn't we feel it move beneath our feet? I have thought a lot about this. Could it be that when you ascended, the Sun dragged you round as it circled the Earth?"

"It is well known," I replied, "that the Sun is a massive body, far bigger than the Earth. Now wouldn't it make sense for our small Earth to orbit the massive Sun, rather than the other way round?"

The Governor though was not convinced, so I continued:

"Consider the stars," I said. "Which is more plausible: that the Earth is static and the distant stars orbit us at what must be a tremendous speed, or that the Earth simply rotates?"

"Well," said the Governor, "I have read somewhere that the damned of Hell climb up from the Earth's core in the vain hope of escaping the terrible flames, and so turn the Earth with their very motion."

So we both agreed that the Earth might revolve, though the Governor seemed a little uneasy with the heretical thought.

"I also believe," said I, stifling a yawn, "that the planets are worlds like ours, and that they too orbit the Sun. But I can go further. The stars we see are distant Suns, and have planets orbiting them. The reason we do not see these planets, is because they are so tiny and emit no light of their own, so we cannot see them."

The Governor pondered this fabulous idea. "If what you say is true, then the beings that inhabit these planets would be able to see more distant stars which also have inhabited planets, and so on, ad infinitum. To think that the Universe might go on forever is mind-boggling. Please go on."

"I think that the Sun purges itself of material that no longer nourishes it, as a fire leaves ashes. This debris is attracted to planets like the Earth either as tiny particles or great lumps, so constantly adding material to our planet. If the Sun emits sufficient material at any one time, this could form a new planet."

The Governor was about to speak but by this point sleep was beginning to overwhelm me, so I bade the Governor goodnight, and my mind filled with dreams of the Moon.

Chapter 4

Setting off for the Moon

For days the Governor and I had many interesting conversations about the planets, stars and the Universe, but in the end the time came when I decided to resume my attempt to reach the Moon.

I first fashioned a wooden contraption with a large pair of wings, and took it up to the top of a nearby hill. With some trepidation I leapt from a rocky outcrop, but instead of gliding through the air, my contraption and I plummeted and tumbled down the hill.

Fortunately I escaped with little more than cuts and bruises. Leaving the contraption behind, I trudged back to my lodgings and cleaned up my wounds. I drank some cordial water, and set off to collect my winged invention, but when I reached the hill I saw, to my horror, that my creation had vanished.

I searched for hours, and eventually came across my invention in the middle of the town square, where a large crowd had gathered round. It transpired that some soldiers had discovered my creation and, realizing that it was meant to fly, had taken it to the square and attached a great number of fireworks to it.

Seeing all the smoke, I thought that they were burning my wooden craft, so I ran forwards, and before anyone could stop me I grabbed the wings. Some soldiers ran towards me, but before they could do anything, I found myself shooting upwards at great speed.

I flew through the clouds, holding on for dear life. Still I continued to head upwards, for hours, and found myself flying towards the Moon. The rockets began to die out and, as I was too tired to hold on much longer my winged contraption fell away from my grasp. Still I continued to fly with the momentum I had been given, and the Moon now was looming large.

For a day and more I flew, and at this point I realized that it was no longer my momentum, but the Moon's gravity, that was pulling me to my destination. Now I was not rising but plummeting towards the new world. Far beneath me, I began to discern all manner of things. But it did not matter – I was resigned to believing that I had no hope of surviving this fall.

The Blazing World (excerpt)

Margaret Cavendish

Introduction

Margaret Cavendish, Duchess of Newcastle-Upon-Tyne (1623–1673) was an English aristocrat with a wide range of activities and interests including writing, animal welfare, philosophy and the issues of gender.

The Blazing World, a portion of which is published here, was first published in 1666, and tells of a woman's journey to the North Pole, where she passes through a gateway into a parallel world. Here she meets an array of strange creatures and even travels in an underwater craft. Much of the science that underpins the story is based on Margaret Cavendish's knowledge of seventeenth century science. This tale is also one of the earliest known tales – perhaps *the* earliest tale – involving parallel worlds.

THE DESCRIPTION OF A NEW WORLD, CALLED The Blazing World,

WRITTEN

By the Thrice Noble, Illustrious, and Excellent PRINCESS,

THE

Duchess of Newcastle.

To The Duchesse of Newcastle, On Her New Blazing World.

Our Elder World, with all their Skill and Arts,
Could but divide the World into three Parts:
Columbus, then for Navigation fam'd,
Found a new World, America 'tis nam'd;
Now this new World was found, it was not made,
Only discovered, lying in Time's shade.

Then what are You, having no Chaos found
To make a World, or any such least ground?
But your Creating Fancy, thought it fit
To make your World of Nothing, but pure Wit.
Your Blazing-World, beyond the Stars mounts higher,
Enlightens all with a Celestial Fire.

William Newcastle.

The Blazing World

Margaret Cavendish

A Merchant travelling into a foreign Country, fell extremely in Love with a young Lady. But being a stranger in that Nation, and beneath her both in Birth and Wealth, he could have but little hopes of obtaining his desire. However, his Love growing more and more vehement upon him, even to the slighting of all difficulties, he resolved at last to Steal her away, which he had the better opportunity to do because her Father's house was not far from the Sea, and she often using to gather shells upon the shore accompanied not with above two to three of her servants, it encouraged him the more to execute his design.

Thus coming one time with a little light Vessel, not unlike a Packet-Boat, manned with some few Seamen, and well victualled for fear of some accidents which might perhaps retard their journey to the place where she used to repair, he forced her away. But when he fancied himself the happiest man of the World, he proved to be the most unfortunate, for Heaven, frowning at his Theft, raised such a Tempest, as they knew not what to do, or whither to steer their course, so that the Vessel, both by its own lightness, and the violent motion of the Wind, was carried as swift as an Arrow out of a Bow, towards the North-pole. And in a short time reached the Icy Sea, where the wind forced it amongst huge pieces of Ice. But being little, and light, it did by the assistance and favour of the Gods to this virtuous Lady, so turn and wind through those precipices, as if it had been guided by some experienced Pilot, and skilful Mariner.

But alas! Those few men which were in it, not knowing whither they went, nor what was to be done in so strange an Adventure, and not being provided for so cold a Voyage, were all frozen to death; the young Lady only, by the light of her Beauty, the heat of her Youth, and Protection of the Gods, remaining alive. Neither was it a wonder that the men did freeze to death, for they were not only driven to the very end or point of the Pole of that World, but even to another Pole of another World, which joined close to it; so that the cold, having a double strength at the conjunction of those two Poles, was insupportable.

At last, the Boat still passing on, was forced into another World, for it is impossible to round this World's Globe from Pole to Pole, so as we do from East to West because the Poles of the other World, joining to the Poles of this, do not allow any further passage to surround the World that way. But if any one arrives to either of these Poles, he is either forced to return, or to enter into another World. And lest you should scruple at it and think if it were thus, those that live at the Poles would either see two Suns at one time, or else they would never want the Sun's light for six months together, as it is commonly believed, you must know that each of these Worlds, having its own Sun to enlighten it, they move each one in their peculiar Circles which motion is so just and exact that neither can hinder or obstruct the other, for they do not exceed their Tropics. And although they should meet, yet we in this World cannot so well perceive them by reason of the brightness of our Sun which, being nearer to us, obstructs the splendor of the Suns of the other World, they being too far off to be discerned by our optic perception, except we use very good Telescopes by which skilful Astronomers have often observed two or three Suns at once.

But to return to the wandering Boat, and the distressed Lady: She, seeing all the Men dead, found small comfort in life. Their Bodies which were preserved all that while from putrefaction and stench by the extremity of cold, began now to thaw and corrupt, whereupon she having not strength enough to fling them over-board, was forced to remove out of her small Cabin, upon the deck, to avoid the nauseous smell. And finding the Boat swim between two plains of Ice, as a stream that runs betwixt two shores, at last perceived land, but covered all with Snow, from which came, walking upon the Ice, strange Creatures, in shape like Bears, only they went upright as men. Those Creatures coming near the Boat, catched hold of it with their Paws that served them instead of hands. Some two or three of them entered first, and when they came out, the rest went in one after another. At last having viewed and observed all that was in the Boat, they spake to each other in a language which the Lady did not understand, and having carried her out of the Boat, sunk it, together with the dead men.

Micromegas

Voltaire

Introduction

François-Marie Arouet, better known as Voltaire (1694–1778) was a prolific French writer and philosopher. His books, letters, pamphlets and other writings number in the tens of thousands.

Micromegas was first published in 1752 and is one of Voltaire's best-known works. The story tells of two giant extraterrestrials who travel across the solar system, eventually reaching the Earth where they meet and enter into a discourse with philosophers. This tale is unusual in that one of the extraterrestrial beings is from a planet orbiting another star. Until this point the aliens of early science fiction had tended to come from within our solar system.

Micromegas

Voltaire

Chapter 1

The Journey of a Being from Sirius to Saturn

On a planet orbiting the star Sirius, there was a young man, some eight miles in height, called Micromegas. Some scholars will calculate that His Excellency, Micromegas, is some twenty-four thousand human steps from head to toe. Now given that we Earthlings aren't much more than five feet, these scholars will realize that Micromegas's world is some twenty-one million six hundred thousand times more voluminous than our tiny planet. Indeed, the difference in size between the states of Germany or Italy, and the mighty empires of Turkey, Russia or China, are as nothing compared to the difference between our planet and that of Micromegas.

With His Excellency, being the height I said, all our sculptors and painters agree that the belt that fits his waist has a length of fifty thousand feet, or to put it another way, his body must have the finest proportions.

As his mind is more cultured than ours, he knows many things. He even made some discoveries of his own when he was barely two hundred and fifty years old, and studying at his planet's Jesuit college. He also solved more than fifty of Euclid's propositions – eighteen more than Blaise Pascal, who, after having solved thirty-two for fun, so his sister said, became a poor surveyor, and an even worse metaphysician.

At the age of about four hundred and fifty, as he emerged from childhood, Micromegas dissected many small insects, some barely a hundred feet in diameter; too small even to be observed through ordinary microscopes.

He also wrote a very interesting book, only to find himself in serious trouble as a result. The Mufti of his country, an ignorant man, viewed the book with suspicion, and thought it pure heresy. The substance of the Mufti's allegation was whether the substantial form of the fleas of Sirius was the same as that of snails. Micromegas gave a spirited defence, and won over the women. The trial lasted two hundred and twenty years, until finally the book was condemned by lawyers who had not read it, and the author was banished from court for eight hundred years.

Micromegas was only moderately upset to be banned by a court that was filled with such pettiness, so he made a very amusing song about the Mufti, and decided to travel from planet to planet, with his companions, to complete his training of heart and mind, as they say.

Those who travel by post-chaise or coach will be surprised by his form of travel, because we, on our little muddy sphere, can scarcely conceive of any other means. Our wonderful traveller knew all the physical laws of attractive and repulsive forces, and made good use of such knowledge. He sometimes used sunbeams, and sometimes made use of comets, travelling from planet to planet, as easily as a bird flies from branch to branch.

Micromegas travelled the breadth of the galaxy in a short time, and I am forced to admit that he never saw the stars that the vicar Derham boasted of having seen through his telescope. Not that I claim that Mr. Derham is a liar – God forbid! Micromegas was there, and a good observer, and I do not wish to contradict anyone.

Micromegas, after his travels about the galaxy, came to the world of Saturn. While he was accustomed to seeing new things, the smallness of the ringed globe and its inhabitants, did make him smile with a sense of superiority that can sometimes even escape the wisest beings. While Saturn is nine hundred times bigger than Earth, compared with His Excellency Micromegas, the citizens of Saturn are mere dwarves, standing a thousand fathoms high or thereabouts.

Micromegas and his companions, did not care for such beings at first, as an Italian musician who visits France might laugh at music of Lully. But as the Sirian had a good spirit, he soon realized that a being need not be laughed at just because he is six thousand feet tall. So, after overcoming his initial surprise, Micromegas befriended the Saturnians. He formed a close friendship with the Secretary of the Academy of Saturn, a man of great wisdom, who had made no discoveries of his own, but who gave a very good account of the discoveries of others.

I shall here, for the satisfaction of readers, relate a strange conversation between Micromegas and the Secretary.

Chapter 2

A Conversation Between the Inhabitants of Sirius and Saturn

After His Excellency, Micromegas, had retired to bed, the Secretary of Saturn paid him a visit.

"I must say," Micromegas mused, "that nature is such a diverse thing."

"Yes," said the Saturnian. "Nature is like a bed with flowers –"

"Ah!" His Excellency exclaimed. "Let us not speak of your flowerbed."

"Then," said the Secretary, "nature resembles an assembly of blondes and brunettes, whose beauty –"

"Oh, what should I care for your brunettes?" said Micromegas.

"Nature is like a gallery of paintings –"

"Oh, no!" said the traveller, "Nature is like nature. Why do you need metaphors?"

"To please you," replied the Secretary.

"I do not want you to please me," replied Micromegas. "I want you to teach me: Pray begin by saying how many senses the men of your world have."

"We have seventy-two, "said the Secretary, "and we complain every day about having so few. Our imagination exceeds our needs, and with our seventy-two senses, five moons and a planetary ring we find ourselves too limited. Despite our curiosity, and our large number of interests that result from our seventy-two senses, we still have plenty of time to get bored."

"I understand," said Micromegas. "In our world we have almost a thousand senses, and we still suffer from a vague, indescribable anxiety, which warns us at every turn that even we are unimportant, and there are many things out there more perfect.

"I travelled a bit, and have seen mortals vastly inferior and vastly superior, but I have seen some who have more desires than true needs, and have more needs than satisfaction. Perhaps, one day, I will find the country where nothing is missing, but so far nobody has informed me of any such place."

The Sirian and Saturnian exhausted themselves with conjecture, but, after much ingenious reasoning they were forced to return to plain facts.

"How long do you live for?" asked the Sirian.

"Oh, not long," replied the man from Saturn.

"It's the same on our world," said the Sirian. "And we always complain, about the life's fleeting existence – it has to be a universal law of nature."

"Alas!" said the Saturnian, "we live a mere five hundred great revolutions of the sun. (Equivalent to fifteen thousand Earth years.) One dies almost as soon as one is born, our existence is a point, an instant in time, and our world is but an atom. No sooner have we begun to learn a little than death comes upon us. For me, I dare not make plans, for I am like a drop of water in a vast ocean. I am ashamed, especially before you, of the ridiculous figure I cut in this world."

Micromegas replied: "If you were not a philosopher, I would fear causing you pain by telling you that our life is seven hundred times longer than yours, but you know too well that when he gives up his body to the elements, nature transforms him into a different state, that we call death, and when that moment of transformation comes, having lived a lifetime, or having lived a day, it is precisely the same thing. I have been in countries where beings live a thousand times longer than me, and I found them lamenting. But everywhere there are sensible people who can accept their lot and thank the Creator. He has created a kind of admirable consistency. For example, while all thinking beings are different, they all are blessed with thoughts and desires. Matter is everywhere, but upon every planet, matter has diverse properties. What properties does matter on Saturn have?"

"If you talk about these properties," said the Saturnian, "without which we believe that this world could not continue as it is, we have three hundred, such as extension, impenetrability, mobility, gravitation, divisibility, and so on."

"Apparently," Micromegas replied, "this small number was ample enough for the Creator when he made your little planet. I admire his wisdom, I see differences everywhere, but everywhere still has a sense of proportion. Your world is small, so are your people, you have some feelings, your matter has some properties, this is the work of Providence. Tell me – what colour is your sun?"

"A strong yellowish white," said the Saturnian, "and when we divide one of its rays, we find that it contains seven colours."

"Our sun glows red," said the Sirian, and its rays are made of thirty-nine primary colours. In my travels, there is no sun, among all those I have passed, that resembles another, just as on your world no two faces are exactly alike."

After several questions of this nature, Micromegas enquired how many substances there were on Saturn. He was told that there were about thirty, like God, space, material, beings who merely feel, beings who feel and think, thinking beings who have no feelings, and so on. The Sirian, astonished the Secretary from Saturn by saying that his distant planet had some three hundred substances, and that furthermore he had discovered another three thousand substances in his travels. Finally, after having communicated to each other a little of what they knew and a lot of what they did not know, and after having reasoned with one another for a Saturnian year, they resolved to make a trip together.

Chapter 3

Our two philosophers, supplied with the finest scientific instruments, were just about to journey up and out of the atmosphere of Saturn, when the Secretary's mistress came to them in tears. She was a small brunette, a mere six hundred and sixty yards in height – but what she lacked in height was more than made up for by her countenance.

"Oh, my cruel love!" she exclaimed, "After fifteen hundred years of resisting you, and now that I finally succumb to your charms, and we have been together barely a hundred years, you leave me to travel with a giant from another world. I see now you were just curious about me, it was not really love. If you were a true Saturnian, you would be faithful. Where are you going? What do you seek? Our five moons wander less than you, and our ring is less changeable. There, I've said it. You know, I'll never love anyone else."

The Secretary embraced her, and wept with her, and the lady, after fainting, went to console herself, and soon took up company with a dandy.

Our two beings left Saturn, taking their servants and instruments with them. They jumped on the first ring, which they found to be quite flat, as had been predicted by a famous inhabitant of Earth, and from here they journeyed from moon to moon. A comet passed quite close to the last satellite, and they leapt onto it.

When they had travelled some hundred and fifty million miles, they arrived at the moons of Jupiter. They went into Jupiter itself, and remained there one year, during which they learned many beautiful secrets that would have been printed in this tale, but for the Inquisition who were appalled by what they read. Still, I was able to read the manuscript in the library of an illustrious Archbishop, who was so kind to let me read his books that I can never thank him sufficiently.

But back to our passengers. Leaving Jupiter, they crossed a space of about a hundred million miles, and they coasted to the planet Mars, which, as we know, is five times smaller than Earth. They saw the two moons that orbit this planet, but which have escaped the notice of our astronomers.

Micromegas and the Secretary found Mars so small that they were afraid of not having enough room to sleep, so they left the planet, as two travellers might bypass a shabby village inn and instead travel on to the next town. But the Sirian and his companion soon began to repent this decision, for they travelled a long time and found nothing. Finally they saw a small glow: it was the Earth: and again they were dismayed by the size of the planet. However, not wishing to decline the chance to rest for a second time, they resolved to land. They leapt onto the tail of a passing comet, and then, seeing an aurora approaching the Earth, used this as a means to descend onto the planet. So they arrived on the north shore of the Baltic Sea, on July 5th 1737.

Chapter 4

What Happened to Them on Earth

After having rested a while, and after their servants had prepared some food, Micromegas and the Secretary ate their lunch off two mountains. Then they decided to explore this small planet, and first travelled southwards. The Sirian's strides, and those of his men, were some thirty-thousand feet in length, and the Saturnian soon found himself panting, and lagging behind, for he had to take twelve steps for every stride of Micromegas. If it is permissible to make such comparisons, their relative size and quickness of pace resembled a tiny lap dog following a Prussian captain of the guards.

The beings were of such a size that they circumnavigated the Earth in thirty-six hours. It is true that the sun orbits the Earth – or more correctly, the Earth rotates on its axis – in a mere twenty four hours, but it must be remembered that is far easier to turn upon an axis than to walk on one's feet. So they returned to the point from which they had left, having observed this almost imperceptible pond, known as the Mediterranean, and that other little pond, known as the Great Ocean. The ocean's surface never reached beyond the Secretary's knee, and it merely lapped at the Micromegas's heel.

During their travels, the two beings did everything they

could to find out whether or not this world was inhabited. They crouched, they lay flat on the ground, and they ran their hands over the Earth's surface, but with their eyes and hands not being commensurate with the smallness of their surroundings, they were unable to detect anything that might make them suspect that we, and all other inhabitants of Earth, exist.

The Secretary, who sometimes came to conclusions a little too fast, soon decided that there was no life on Earth. He reasoned this on the grounds that he had seen anyone. In a polite manner, Micromegas said that this was poor logic: "Because," he said, "your small eyes do not see some distant stars that I see very distinctly, would you conclude that these stars do not exist?"

"But," said the Secretary, "I have also used my sense of touch to feel for life."

"But your sense of touch is hardly suitable for the subtleties of this terrain," Micromegas replied.

The Secretary from Saturn objected. "This planet is so poorly constructed; it is irregular, and has a form that seems so ridiculous! Everything here seems to be chaotic. Look at the small streams, and how they meander in such an irregular fashion. And these ponds – they're neither round, nor square, or oval, or any regular shape. And what about all these jagged spikes that stick out the ground and scratch our feet? (He meant the mountains.) Do you notice that this globe isn't even a perfect sphere? It's flat at the poles, and it orbits the sun in such a way that causes the climates of the poles to remain cold and inhospitable? I don't think anyone with a drop of common sense would stay here."

"Well," said Micromegas, "Perhaps this planet is inhabited by people who aren't sensible. But there are indications that this planet was created for a purpose. Everything on this globe appears to be irregular, you say, because on Jupiter and Saturn everything is done with precision. But haven't I said that in my travels I have always noticed great variety?"

The Saturnian replied to all the Sirian's arguments, and it seemed the dispute would never finish, but fortunately Micromegas, when warming up to speak, broke the thread of his diamond necklace. The diamonds, pretty and small, fell, the largest weighing four hundred pounds and the smallest a mere fifty. As the Secretary picked some up, he noticed that because of the way these diamonds were cut, they acted as excellent microscopes. He took one diamond, some one hundred and sixty feet in diameter, and peered through it. Micromegas also took a diamond some two thousand five hundred feet in diameter. The diamonds made excellent viewing instruments, but first the two beings saw nothing and it was necessary to adjust their diamond lenses. Finally the being from Saturn saw something moving, almost imperceptibly, under the surface of the Baltic Sea – it was a whale. The Secretary scooped it from the water with a finger, and placed it on his thumbnail. Then he showed the Sirian, who laughed at the excessive smallness of this Earthly inhabitant. The Saturnian, was now convinced that our world was inhabited and imagined it was populated only by whales. As he was great reasoner, he tried to guess how it moved, and whether or not so tiny a creature might have ideas, desires and freedom.

Micromegas examined the animal patiently, and concluded that this animal could not possibly have a soul. The two travellers were inclined therefore to think that there was no intelligent life on Earth, when through a microscope, they saw something as big as a whale floating on the Baltic Sea. It happened to be a flock of philosophers returning from the Arctic Circle, which they had recently visited in the hope of making new discoveries. The newspapers of the day said that this ship ran aground on the coast of Bothnia, that they had great difficulty in escaping, and that what really happened will never be known. I, however, will tell you exactly what happened, and without embellishment – which is no small effort for a historian.

Chapter 5

Experience and Reasoning of the Two Travellers

Micromegas extended his hand slowly toward the spot where the object appeared, and advancing two shaking fingers, he adroitly seized the ship that carried these gentlemen, and, without too much pressure for fear of crushing it, he placed it on his fingertip.

"This is a very different animal from the first," said the Saturnian.

Micromegas put the animal in the hollow of his hand. The terrified passengers and crew, believed they had been swept up by a hurricane, and believed themselves to have come to rest on some sort of rock. Frightened by their ordeal, the sailors lifted wine barrels, and threw them onto the palm of Micromegas, and quickly followed their cargo.

Surveyors took their most valued items – quadrants, sextants, and Lapp girls – and they descended onto one of the Sirian's fingers. At first the giant being felt nothing, and then a slight tickling a finger – a stake had been hammered into his skin. Micromegas judged by the tingling, that this was the doing of the small animal he had in his palm. The microscope, which was barely able to discern a whale from a ship, had not the power to pick out things as insignificant as men. I do not pretend to shock anyone's vanity, but I am compelled to point out that by taking the average height of man as being standing five feet on this Earth, if our planet were ten feet in circumference, we would be a mere six hundred thousandth of an inch in height. Imagine a being, with organs like ours, and who could hold the Earth in his hand, and such creatures may well exist. I ask you: what they would think of these battles where we capture a couple of villages, only to lose them again in the next battle?

I have no doubt that if any captain of grenadiers ever reads this tale, he might well increase the height of his soldier's caps by a good two feet. But I must warn him that even if he does this, he and his men will always remain infinitely small.

What marvellous skill then, did it take for our philosopher Micromegas to finally see these minute creatures that I just mentioned? When Leuwenhoek and Hartsoeker first peered down their microscopes to see the seeds from which we are all born, they were not as astonished as Micromegas was when he saw humans for the first time. Micromegas felt great pleasure upon seeing these little machines move. He watched their actions and followed their every move! He cried with joy as he put a microscope in the hands of his travelling companion.

"I see them," they said in unison. "Do not you see them carrying their burdens?"

As they spoke of the pleasure of seeing objects so new, their hands trembled excitedly, and they feared losing the tiny beings. The Saturnian, switching from an excess of confidence to an excess of credulity, thought he saw some of the creatures making love.

"Ah," he said, "I am seeing nature at work."

But he was deceived by appearances; something that happens whether we use microscopes or not.

Chapter 6

What happened to Them in the Company of Men

Micromegas, a much better observer than the Secretary, clearly saw that the creatures were talking, and he remarked to his companion, who, ashamed of having mistakenly believed what he was witnessing a moment ago, now could not believe that such a tiny species was capable of communication. The Saturnian spoke many languages, and reasoned that as he could not hear these atom-sized beings speak, they did not speak. Furthermore, he reasoned, how could these imperceptible organs have voices, and what would such insignificant creatures have to say? If they could speak then they had to think, and if they could think then surely they must have souls. But to the Secretary, the idea that such puny creatures might have souls seemed absurd.

"Earlier you thought they were making love," reasoned Micromegas. "Do you think one can make love without thinking, and without uttering a word? Do you suppose it is more difficult to produce an argument than a child? For me, both are great mysteries."

"I neither believe nor deny, "said the Saturnian. "I have no opinion. We must try to examine these insects".

"Well said," Micromegas replied, and he pulled a pair of scissors and a trimmed his thumbnail. He made, in no time, a kind of great trumpet like a vast funnel, and he put the narrower end to his ear. The circumference of the funnel enveloped the ship and the crew. The weakest voice entered the circular fibres of the trumpet, so that Micromegas heard a sound that resembled the buzzing of insects.

In a few hours he managed to distinguish the words, and finally to hear French. The Secretary did the same, although with more difficulty, and the astonishment of the travellers grew. What Micromegas and the Secretary heard made good sense. The Saturnian burned with impatience to enter into conversation with the atom-sized beings, but feared that his thunderous voice, and especially that of Micromegas, might deafen them. They had to reduce the volume, so they fashioned a device resembling small toothpick, placing one end in their mouths and the other end close to the ship. The Sirian placed the Secretary on his knees, and places the ship and her crew on his fingernail. Micromegas bowed his head and spoke softly. Finally, with all these precautions, and many others, he began his speech:

"Invisible insects to whom the Creator has given life, in the abyss of the infinitely small, I appreciate that he has deigned me to discover secrets that might otherwise have seemed impenetrable. Maybe my kind would not even deign to look at you, but I do not despise anyone, and I offer you my protection."

If ever anyone was surprised, it was the people who heard these words, and they could not guess where they came from. The ship's chaplain recited prayers for exorcism, the sailors swore, and the philosophers of the ship discussed the matter and swiftly concluded that they would never discover who had spoken to them. The Saturnian, who had a softer voice than Micromegas, then told the tiny beings what species they were dealing. He told them of the trip from Saturn, and told them of Micromegas. After pitying them for being so small, he asked them if they had always been in this miserable state of insignificance, what they did in a world that seemed to belong to whales, if they were happy, if they procreated, if they had a soul, and a hundred other questions of this nature.

One crew member, bolder than the others, and shocked that anyone could doubt he had a soul, observed the speaker with the sight of his quadrant, made three measurements, then spoke:

"You think then, sir, because you are thousand yards from head to toe, you are a –"

"A thousand yards!" cried the Secretary. "Heaven! How can he know my height? A thousand yards! He's accurate to one iota. I've been measured by an atom! He is a surveyor who knows my size, and I, who see only through a microscope, I could not even fathom his!"

"Yes, I've measured you," said the physicist, "and, if I may, I would like to measure your great companion too."

The proposal was accepted, and His Excellency lay down, for, had he remained standing, his head would have been far above the clouds. The ship's philosophers planted a large tree in a part of Micromagas's anatomy that Dr. Swift would happily name, but I shall not mention out of respect for the ladies. Then, by a series of triangles linked together, they concluded that what they saw was a young man, some one hundred twenty thousand feet from head to toe.

Then Micromegas uttered these words: "I see more than ever that we should not judge anything by its size. O, God! who gave intelligence to substances that seem so insignificant, the infinitely small takes you as little effort as infinitely large and, if it is possible, I wonder that there are things still smaller than them, things that might have a spirit greater even than those beautiful animals I've seen during my travels, creatures of greater size than the planet where I now stand."

A philosopher replied that there were indeed intelligent creatures much smaller than man. He told him, not of Virgil's fabulous account of bees, but of what Swammerdam had discovered, and what Reaumur had dissected. Micromegas finally learned that there are animals that are to bees what bees are to humans, and though Micromegas himself was tiny compared to the planet-sized animals he had earlier mentioned, these large animals might appear to others to be mere atoms.

Soon the conversation became interesting and Micromegas spoke well.

Chapter 7

"Intelligent atoms, through which the Eternal Being has demonstrated his skill and power, I imagine you taste much joy in your world, with such tiny bodies, and great minds, you must spend a lifetime loving and thinking, and living the true life of the spirits. I have seen true happiness nowhere else, but here it is, without doubt."

At these words the philosophers shook their heads, and one of them, more frank than the others admitted that except for a small number of people, everyone else was a blend of mad, bad and unhappy.

"If evil is something that is born of matter, then even we, with our small size, have more material than we need," he said, "and if evil comes from the mind, then we are certainly too clever. For example, as I speak, there are a hundred thousand fools, wearing hats, either killing, or being killed by a hundred thousand fools wearing turbans. This happens across the world, and has happened since time immemorial."

Micromegas shuddered, and asked what caused these quarrels.

"The battle of which I speak," said the philosopher, "is over a pile of mud the size of your heel. Not one of these millions of men who kill lay claim to so much as a single straw on that pile of mud. Instead they fight on behalf of a man called Sultan, or another called the Tzar. Neither

Sultan nor Tzar has ever seen, and will never see, the little patch of land in question, and almost none of these animals who slay each other, will see the animal in whose name they slay."

"How terrible!" exclaimed the Sirian, "I can barely comprehend such a frenzied fit of rage! I want to take three strides and crush this swarm of assassins with each step."

"Don't bother," the philosophers replied, "They're doing a good enough job themselves. After ten years, not a hundredth of these wretches survive – even if they have not drawn a sword, for hunger and fatigue carry them off. Moreover, it is not they who should be punished, but the barbarians far from the battlefield who, between hearty meals, order the massacre of a million men, and then solemnly thank God."

The traveller pitied the human race, in which he discovered such amazing contrasts. "Since you are among the small number of Wise Men," said Micromegas, "and do not kill for money, pray tell me what you care for most."

"We dissect flies," said a philosopher, "we measure lines, we add numbers, we agree on two or three points that we understand, and we argue over two or three thousand that we do not."

The Sirian and Saturnian asked the beings, to tell them what things they agreed upon.

"What is the distance," he said, "From the Dog Star to the largest star in the constellation of Gemini?"

The philosophers all answered at once: "thirty-two and a half degrees."

"How far away is the Moon?"

"Approximately sixty times the radius of the Earth."

"How heavy is your air?"

He believed he had caught them out, but they all told him that air weighs about nine hundred times less than the same volume of water, and nine hundred to a thousand times less than gold used for ducats. The Secretary was astonished by their answers, and while had refused them souls quarter of an hour ago, he was now tempted to believe they were witches.

Finally Micromegas said: "Since you know so well what is outside you, you probably know better what lies inside you. Tell me about your soul, and how you form your ideas."

The philosophers began to talk, and all had different answers. The oldest quoted Aristotle, one mentioned Descartes, another talked of Malebranche, another of Leibnitz, and another still spoke of Locke.

A confident old Peripatetic said aloud: "The soul is an entelechy, and this is the reason for which it has the power to be what it is. This is what Aristotle says expressly, on page 633 of the Louvre edition. Ἐντελεχεῖα ἐστι..."'

"I do not understand Greek very well," Micromegas interrupted.

"Nor I," said the philosophical being.

"Well then," asked the Sirian, "why do you quote Aristotle in Greek?"

"Because," said the scientist, "one must always quote something one does not understand in the language one understands the least."

The Cartesian came in at this point and said, "The soul is

a pure spirit who, when in the womb absorbs all metaphysical ideas, and on leaving the womb, is forced to go to school, and learn anew what it once knew so well."

"So your soul was learned in the womb," said Micromegas, "but you became more ignorant as you developed a beard on your chin. What do you mean by 'spirit'?"

"I have no idea," came the reply. "They say that the spirit is not the same as matter."

"Do you know then what matter is?"

"I do," replied the man. "For example, this stone is grey, it has three dimensions, it is heavy, and divisible."

"Well!" said the Sirian, that thing that you seem to be divisible, heavy and grey, would you tell me what it is? You see a few attributes, but can you tell me the essential substance of the thing?"

"No," said the Cartesian.

"Then you do not you know matter is."

Micromegas now addressed himself to another wise man who stood on his thumb, and asked him what his soul was like, and what it did.

"Nothing," replied the philosopher of Malebranche, "God does everything for me. I do everything through him. He does everything without my help."

"One might as well not exist," said Micromegas. "And what of you, my friend," he said to a Leibnitzian who was there. "What is your soul?"

"It, is the hand that shows the time while my body chimes," said the Leibnitzian, "or, if you will, my soul chimes while my body shows the time, or, it could be said, my soul is the mirror of the universe, and my body is the edge of the mirror."

A small supporter of Locke waited close by, and when he was finally asked of his soul by Micromegas, he replied: "I do not know how I think, but I know I never thought without the use of my senses. I don't doubt that there exist intelligent ethereal substances, but I don't believe it is impossible for God to bestow mind to matter. I revere the eternal power and it is not for me to limit it: I affirm nothing, I just believe that there are more things possible than we think."

The Sirian smiled. He did not find this person the least wise, and the Saturnian would have embraced the follower of Locke but for their extreme disparity. There was, however, a human with a square cap who spoke out to the giant beings. He said he knew all the answers they had sought, and that these answers could be found in the Summa of St. Thomas. He looked up at the two giants and argued that they, their worlds, their suns, their stars, and indeed everything was done purely for the benefit of mankind.

The two travellers had to hold one another are they tried in vain to stifle their laughter. Their shoulders and bellies shook, and with their convulsions, the microscopic ship and her crew fell from the Micromegas's hand and into one of the Secretary's trouser pockets. These two good people searched and eventually found the crew. The Sirian picked up the small beings, and spoke kindly to them, even though he was a little angry to see that these almost infinitesimally small beings had a pride that was almost infinitely great.

At length Micromegas promised to give them a good philosophy book, written especially for their use, and that this book, would tell them of the very nature of all things. Indeed, he gave them this volume before his departure, and the book was taken at once to the Academy of Sciences in Paris, but when the official at the Academy opened it, he saw the book of answers contained only blank pages.

"Yes," he said, "It is just as I thought!"

The Unparalleled Adventure of One Hans Pfaall

Edgar Allan Poe

Introduction

Edgar Allan Poe (1809–1849), was born in Boston, Massachusetts and is best remembered for his Gothic tales. He was however also highly influential in the genres of early detective and science fiction, influencing the likes of Sir Arthur Conan Doyle and Jules Verne.

The Unparalleled Adventure of One Hans Pfaall was first published in the *Southern Literary Messenger* in June 1835. Presenting it as a true account, Poe intended the story to be a hoax. The tale tells of Hans Pfaall's journey to the Moon by hot air balloon, and gives an account of how he survived travelling through the vacuum of space. It is likely that the story was influenced by Francis Godwin's *The Man in the Moone*, which Poe discusses in some detail in the *Commentary* at the end of the story. Perhaps *The Unparalleled Adventure*'s greatest contribution to early science fiction was it's influence on Jules Verne's classic science fiction tale *From the Earth to the Moon*.

The Unparalleled Adventure of One Hans Pfaall

Edgar Allan Poe

By late accounts from Rotterdam, that city seems to be in a high state of philosophical excitement. Indeed, phenomena have there occurred of a nature so completely unexpected — so entirely novel — so utterly at variance with preconceived opinions — as to leave no doubt on my mind that long ere this all Europe is in an uproar, all physics in a ferment, all reason and astronomy together by the ears.

It appears that on the __ day of __ (I am not positive about the date), a vast crowd of people, for purposes not specifically mentioned, were assembled in the great square of the Exchange in the well-conditioned city of Rotterdam. The day was warm — unusually so for the season — there was hardly a breath of air stirring; and the multitude were in no bad humor at being now and then besprinkled with friendly showers of momentary duration, that fell from large white masses of cloud which chequered in a fitful manner the blue vault of the firmament. Nevertheless, about noon, a slight but remarkable agitation became apparent in the assembly: the clattering of ten thousand tongues succeeded; and, in an instant afterward, ten thousand faces were upturned toward the heavens, ten thousand pipes descended simultaneously from the corners of ten thousand mouths, and a shout, which could be compared to nothing but the roaring of Niagara, resounded long, loudly, and furiously, through all the environs of Rotterdam.

The origin of this hubbub soon became sufficiently evident. From behind the huge bulk of one of those sharply-defined masses of cloud already mentioned, was seen slowly to emerge into an open area of blue space, a queer, heterogeneous, but apparently solid substance, so oddly shaped, so whimsically put together, as not to be in any manner comprehended, and never to be sufficiently admired, by the host of sturdy burghers who stood open-mouthed below. What could it be? In the name of all the vrows and devils in Rotterdam, what could it possibly portend? No one knew, no one could imagine; no one — not even the burgomaster Mynheer Superbus Von Underduk — had the slightest clew by which to unravel the mystery; so, as nothing more reasonable could be done, every one to a man replaced his pipe carefully in the corner of his mouth, and cocking up his right eye towards the phenomenon, puffed, paused, waddled about, and grunted significantly — then waddled back, grunted, paused, and finally — puffed again.

In the meantime, however, lower and still lower toward the goodly city, came the object of so much curiosity, and the cause of so much smoke. In a very few minutes it arrived near enough to be accurately discerned. It appeared to be — yes! it was undoubtedly a species of balloon; but surely no such balloon had ever been seen in Rotterdam before. For who, let me ask, ever heard of a balloon manufactured entirely of dirty newspapers? No man in Holland certainly; yet here, under the very noses of the people, or rather at some distance above their noses was the identical thing in question, and composed, I have it on the best authority, of the precise material which no one had ever before known to be used for a similar purpose. It was an egregious insult to the good sense of the burghers of Rotterdam. As to the shape of the phenomenon, it was even still more reprehensible. Being little or nothing better than a huge foolscap turned upside down. And this similitude was regarded as by no means lessened when, upon nearer inspection, there was perceived a large tassel depending from its apex, and, around the upper rim or base of the cone, a circle of little instruments, resembling sheep-bells, which kept up a continual tinkling to the tune of Betty Martin. But still worse. Suspended by blue ribbons to the end of this fantastic machine, there hung, by way of car, an enormous drab beaver bat, with a brim superlatively broad, and a hemispherical crown with a black band and a silver buckle. It is, however, somewhat remarkable that many citizens of Rotterdam swore to having seen the same hat repeatedly before; and indeed the whole assembly seemed to regard it with eyes of familiarity; while the vrow Grettel Pfaall, upon sight of it, uttered an exclamation of joyful surprise, and declared it to be the identical hat of her good man himself. Now this was a circumstance the more to be observed, as Pfaall, with three companions, had actually disappeared from Rotterdam about five years before, in a very sudden and unaccountable manner, and up to the date of this narrative all attempts had failed of obtaining any intelligence concerning them whatsoever. To be sure, some bones which were thought to be human, mixed up with a quantity of odd-looking rubbish, had been lately discovered in a retired situation to the east of Rotterdam, and some people went so far as to imagine that in this spot a foul murder had been committed, and that the sufferers were in all probability Hans Pfaall and his associates. But to return.

The balloon (for such no doubt it was) had now descended to within a hundred feet of the earth, allowing the crowd below a sufficiently distinct view of the person of its occupant. This was in truth a very droll little somebody. He could not have been more than two feet in height; but this altitude, little as it was, would have been sufficient to destroy his equilibrium, and tilt him over the edge of his tiny car, but for the intervention of a circular rim reaching as high as the breast, and rigged on to the cords of the balloon. The body of the little man was more than proportionately broad, giving to his entire figure a rotundity highly absurd. His feet, of course, could not be seen at all, although a horny substance of suspicious nature was occasionally protruded through a rent in the bottom of the car, or to speak more properly, in the top of the hat.

His hands were enormously large. His hair was extremely gray, and collected in a cue behind. His nose was prodigiously long, crooked, and inflammatory; his eyes full, brilliant, and acute; his chin and cheeks, although wrinkled with age, were broad, puffy, and double; but of ears of any kind or character there was not a semblance to be discovered upon any portion of his head. This odd little gentleman was dressed in a loose surtout of sky-blue satin, with tight breeches to match, fastened with silver buckles at the knees. His vest was of some bright yellow material; a white taffety cap was set jauntily on one side of his head; and, to complete his equipment, a blood-red silk handkerchief enveloped his throat, and fell down, in a dainty manner, upon his bosom, in a fantastic bow-knot of super-eminent dimensions.

Having descended, as I said before, to about one hundred feet from the surface of the earth, the little old gentleman was suddenly seized with a fit of trepidation, and appeared disinclined to make any nearer approach to terra firma. Throwing out, therefore, a quantity of sand from a canvas bag, which, he lifted with great difficulty, he became stationary in an instant. He then proceeded, in a hurried and agitated manner, to extract from a side-pocket in his surtout a large morocco pocket-book. This he poised suspiciously in his hand, then eyed it with an air of extreme surprise, and was evidently astonished at its weight. He at length opened it, and drawing there from a huge letter sealed with red sealing wax and tied carefully with red tape, let it fall precisely at the feet of the burgomaster, Superbus Von Underduk. His Excellency stooped to take it up. But the aeronaut, still greatly discomposed, and having apparently no farther business to detain him in Rotterdam, began at this moment to make busy preparations for departure; and it being necessary to discharge a portion of ballast to enable him to reascend, the half dozen bags which he threw out, one after another, without taking the trouble to empty their contents, tumbled, every one of them, most unfortunately upon the back of the burgomaster, and rolled him over and over no less than one-and-twenty times, in the face of every man in Rotterdam. It is not to be supposed, however, that the great Underduk suffered this impertinence on the part of the little old man to pass off with impunity. It is said, on the contrary, that during each and every one of his one-and twenty circumvolutions he emitted no less than one-and-twenty distinct and furious whiffs from his pipe, to which he held fast the whole time with all his might, and to which he intends holding fast until the day of his death.

In the meantime the balloon arose like a lark, and, soaring far away above the city, at length drifted quietly behind a cloud similar to that from which it had so oddly emerged, and was thus lost forever to the wondering eyes of the good citizens of Rotterdam. All attention was now directed to the letter, the descent of which, and the consequences attending thereupon, had proved so fatally subversive of both person and personal dignity to his Excellency, the illustrious Burgomaster Mynheer Superbus Von Underduk. That functionary, however, had not failed, during his circumgyratory movements, to bestow a thought upon the important subject of securing the packet in question, which was seen, upon inspection, to have fallen into the most proper hands, being actually addressed to himself and Professor Rub-a-dub, in their official capacities of President and Vice-President of the Rotterdam College of Astronomy. It was accordingly opened by those dignitaries upon the spot, and found to contain the following extraordinary, and indeed very serious, communications.

To their Excellencies Von Underduk and Rub-a-dub, President and Vice-President of the States' College of

Astronomers, in the city of Rotterdam.

Your Excellencies may perhaps be able to remember an humble artizan, by name Hans Pfaall, and by occupation a mender of bellows, who, with three others, disappeared from Rotterdam, about five years ago, in a manner which must have been considered by all parties at once sudden, and extremely unaccountable. If, however, it so please your excellencies, I, the writer of this communication, am the identical Hans Pfaall himself. It is well known to most of my fellow citizens, that for the period of forty years I continued to occupy the little square brick building, at the head of the alley called Sauerkraut, in which I resided at the time of my disappearance. My ancestors have also resided therein time out of mind — they, as well as myself, steadily following the respectable and indeed lucrative profession of mending of bellows. For, to speak the truth, until of late years, that the heads of all the people have been set agog with politics, no better business than my own could an honest citizen of Rotterdam either desire or deserve. Credit was good, employment was never wanting, and on all hands there was no lack of either money or good-will. But, as I was saying, we soon began to feel the effects of liberty and long speeches, and radicalism, and all that sort of thing. People who were formerly, the very best customers in the world, had now not a moment of time to think of us at all. They had, so they said, as much as they could do to read about the revolutions, and keep up with the march of intellect and the spirit of the age. If a fire wanted fanning, it could readily be fanned with a newspaper, and as the government grew weaker, I have no doubt that leather and iron acquired durability in proportion, for, in a very short time, there was not a pair of bellows in all Rotterdam that ever stood in need of a stitch or required the assistance of a hammer. This was a state of things not to be endured. I soon grew as poor as a rat, and, having a wife and children to provide for, my burdens at length became intolerable, and I spent hour after hour in reflecting upon the most convenient method of putting an end to my life. Duns, in the meantime, left me little leisure for contemplation. My house was literally besieged from morning till night, so that I began to rave, and foam, and fret like a caged tiger against the bars of his enclosure. There were three fellows in particular who worried me beyond endurance, keeping watch continually about my door, and threatening me with the law. Upon these three I internally vowed the bitterest revenge, if ever I should be so happy as to get them within my clutches; and I believe nothing in the world but the pleasure of this anticipation prevented me from putting my plan of suicide into immediate execution, by blowing my brains out with a blunderbuss. I thought it best, however, to dissemble my wrath, and to treat them with promises and fair words, until, by some good turn of fate, an opportunity of vengeance should be afforded me.

One day, having given my creditors the slip, and feeling more than usually dejected, I continued for a long time to wander about the most obscure streets without object whatever, until at length I chanced to stumble against the corner of a bookseller's stall. Seeing a chair close at hand, for the use of customers, I threw myself doggedly into it, and, hardly knowing why, opened the pages of the first volume which came within my reach. It proved to be a small pamphlet treatise on Speculative Astronomy, written either by Professor Encke of Berlin or by a Frenchman of somewhat similar name. I had some little tincture of information on matters of this nature, and soon became more and more absorbed in the contents of the book, reading it actually through twice before I awoke to a recollection of what was passing around me. By this time it began to grow dark, and I directed my steps toward home. But the treatise had made an indelible impression on my mind, and, as I sauntered along the dusky streets, I revolved carefully over in my memory the wild and sometimes unintelligible reasonings of the writer. There are some particular passages which affected my imagination in a powerful and extraordinary manner. The longer I meditated upon these the more intense grew the interest which had been excited within me. The limited nature of my education in general, and more especially my ignorance on subjects connected with natural philosophy, so far from rendering me diffident of my own ability to comprehend what I had read, or inducing me to mistrust the many vague notions which had arisen in consequence, merely served as a farther stimulus to imagination; and I was vain enough, or perhaps reasonable enough, to doubt whether those crude ideas which, arising in ill-regulated minds, have all the appearance, may not often in effect possess all the force, the reality, and other inherent properties, of instinct or intuition; whether, to proceed a step farther, profundity itself might not, in matters of a purely speculative nature, be detected as a legitimate source of falsity and error. In other words, I believed, and still do believe, that truth, is frequently of its own essence, superficial, and that, in many cases, the depth lies more in the abysses where we seek her, than in the actual situations wherein she may be found. Nature herself seemed to afford me corroboration of these ideas. In the contemplation of the heavenly bodies it struck me forcibly that I could not distinguish a star with nearly as much precision, when I gazed on it with earnest, direct and undeviating attention, as when I suffered my eye only to glance in its vicinity alone. I was not, of course, at that time aware that this apparent paradox was occasioned by the center of the visual area being less susceptible of feeble impressions of light than the exterior portions of the retina. This knowledge, and some of another kind, came afterwards in the course of an eventful five years, during which I have dropped the prejudices of my former humble situation in life, and forgotten the bellows-mender in far different occupations. But at the epoch of which I speak, the analogy which a casual observation of a star offered to the conclusions I had already drawn, struck me with the force of positive conformation, and I then finally made up my mind to the course which I afterwards pursued.

It was late when I reached home, and I went immediately to bed. My mind, however, was too much occupied to sleep, and I lay the whole night buried in meditation. Arising early in the morning, and contriving again to escape the vigilance of my creditors, I repaired eagerly to the bookseller's stall, and laid out what little ready money I possessed, in the purchase of some volumes of Mechanics and Practical Astronomy. Having arrived at home safely with these, I devoted every spare moment to their perusal, and soon made such proficiency in studies of this nature as I thought sufficient for the execution of my plan. In the intervals of this period, I made every endeavor to conciliate the three creditors who had given me so much annoyance. In this I finally succeeded — partly by selling enough of my household furniture to satisfy a moiety of their claim, and partly by a promise of paying the balance upon completion of a little project which I told them I had in view, and for assistance in which I solicited their services. By these means — for they were ignorant men — I found little difficulty in gaining them over to my purpose.

Matters being thus arranged, I contrived, by the aid of my wife and with the greatest secrecy and caution, to dispose of what property I had remaining, and to borrow, in small sums, under various pretences, and without paying any attention to my future means of repayment, no inconsiderable quantity of ready money. With the means thus accruing I proceeded to procure at intervals, cambric muslin, very fine, in pieces of twelve yards each; twine; a lot of the varnish of caoutchouc; a large and deep basket of wicker-work, made to order; and several other articles necessary in the construction and equipment of a balloon of extraordinary dimensions. This I directed my wife to make up as soon as possible, and gave her all requisite information as to the particular method of proceeding. In the meantime I worked up the twine into a net-work of sufficient dimensions; rigged it with a hoop and the necessary cords; bought a quadrant, a compass, a spy-glass, a common barometer with some important modifications, and two astronomical instruments not so generally known. I then took opportunities of conveying by night, to a retired situation east of Rotterdam, five iron-bound casks, to contain about fifty gallons each, and one of a larger size; six tinned ware tubes, three inches in diameter, properly shaped, and ten feet in length; a quantity of a particular metallic substance, or semi-metal, which I shall not name, and a dozen demijohns of a very common acid. The gas to be formed from these latter materials is a gas never yet generated by any other person than myself — or at least never applied to any similar purpose. The secret I would make no difficulty in disclosing, but that it of right belongs to a citizen of Nantz, in France, by whom it was conditionally communicated to myself. The same individual submitted to me, without being at all aware of my intentions, a method of constructing balloons from the membrane of a certain animal, through which substance any escape of gas was nearly an impossibility. I found it, however, altogether too expensive, and was not sure, upon the whole, whether cambric muslin with a coating of gum caoutchouc, was not equally as good. I mention this circumstance, because I think it probable that hereafter the individual in question may attempt a balloon ascension with the novel gas and material I have spoken of, and I do not wish to deprive him of the honor of a very singular invention.

On the spot which I intended each of the smaller casks to occupy respectively during the inflation of the balloon, I privately dug a hole two feet deep; the holes forming in this manner a circle twenty-five feet in diameter. In the centre of this circle, being the station designed for the large cask, I also dug a hole three feet in depth. In each of the five smaller holes, I deposited a canister containing fifty pounds, and in the larger one a keg holding one hundred and fifty pounds, of cannon powder. These — the keg and canisters — I connected in a proper manner with covered trains; and having let into one of the canisters the end of about four feet of slow match, I covered up the hole, and placed the cask over it, leaving the other end of the match protruding about an inch, and barely visible beyond the cask. I then filled up the remaining holes, and placed the barrels over them in their destined situation.

Besides the articles above enumerated, I conveyed to the depot, and there secreted, one of M. Grimm's improvements upon the apparatus for condensation of the atmospheric air. I found this machine, however, to require considerable alteration before it could be adapted to the purposes to which I intended making it applicable. But, with severe labor and unremitting perseverance, I at length met with entire success in all my preparations. My balloon was soon completed. It would contain more than forty thousand cubic feet of gas; would take me up easily, I calculated, with all my implements, and, if I managed rightly, with one hundred and seventy-five pounds of ballast into the bargain. It had received three coats of varnish, and I found the cambric muslin to answer all the purposes of silk itself, quite as strong and a good deal less expensive.

Everything being now ready, I exacted from my wife an oath of secrecy in relation to all my actions from the day of my first visit to the bookseller's stall; and promising, on my part, to return as soon as circumstances would permit, I gave her what little money I had left, and bade her farewell. Indeed I had no fear on her account. She was what people call a notable woman, and could manage matters in the world without my assistance. I believe, to tell the truth, she always looked upon me as an idle boy, a mere make-weight, good for nothing but building castles in the air, and was rather glad to get rid of me. It was a dark night when I bade her good-bye, and taking with me, as aides-de-camp, the three creditors who had given me so much trouble, we carried the balloon, with the car and accoutrements, by a roundabout way, to the station where the other articles were deposited. We there found them all unmolested, and I proceeded immediately to business.

It was the first of April. The night, as I said before, was dark; there was not a star to be seen; and a drizzling rain, falling at intervals, rendered us very uncomfortable. But my chief anxiety was concerning the balloon, which, in spite of the varnish with which it was defended, began to grow rather heavy with the moisture; the powder also was liable to damage. I therefore kept my three duns working with great diligence, pounding down ice around the central cask, and stirring the acid in the others. They did not cease, however, importuning me with questions as to what I intended to do with all this apparatus, and expressed much dissatisfaction at the terrible labor I made them undergo. They could not perceive, so they said, what good was likely to result from their getting wet to the skin, merely to take a part in such horrible incantations. I began to get uneasy, and worked away with all my might, for I verily believe the idiots supposed that I had entered into a compact with the devil, and that, in short, what I was now doing was nothing better than it should be. I was, therefore, in great fear of their leaving me altogether. I contrived, however, to pacify them by promises of payment of all scores in full, as soon as I could bring the present business to a termination. To these speeches they gave, of course, their own interpretation; fancying, no doubt, that at all events I should come into possession of vast quantities of ready money; and provided I paid them all I owed, and a trifle more, in consideration of their services, I dare say they cared very little what became of either my soul or my carcass.

In about four hours and a half I found the balloon sufficiently inflated. I attached the car, therefore, and put all my implements in it — not forgetting the condensing apparatus, a copious supply of water, and a large quantity of provisions, such as pemmican, in which much nutriment is contained in comparatively little bulk. I also secured in the car a pair of pigeons and a cat. It was now nearly daybreak, and I thought it high time to take my departure. Dropping a lighted cigar on the ground, as if by accident, I took the opportunity, in stooping to pick it up, of igniting privately the piece of slow match, whose end, as I said before, protruded a very little beyond the lower rim of one of the smaller casks. This manoeuvre was totally unperceived on the part of the three duns; and, jumping into the car, I immediately cut the single cord which held me to the earth, and was pleased to find that I shot upward, carrying with all ease one hundred and seventy-five pounds of leaden ballast, and able to have carried up as many more.

Scarcely, however, had I attained the height of fifty yards, when, roaring and rumbling up after me in the most horrible and tumultuous manner, came so dense a hurricane of fire, and smoke, and sulphur, and legs and arms, and gravel, and burning wood, and blazing metal, that my very heart sunk within me, and I fell down in the bottom of the car, trembling with unmitigated terror. Indeed, I now perceived that I had entirely overdone the business, and that the main consequences of the shock were yet to be experienced. Accordingly, in less than a second, I felt all the blood in my body rushing to my temples, and immediately thereupon, a concussion, which I shall never forget, burst abruptly through the night and seemed to rip the very firmament asunder. When I afterward had time for reflection, I did not fail to attribute the extreme violence of the explosion, as regarded myself, to its proper cause — my situation directly above it, and in the line of its greatest power. But at the time, I thought only of preserving my life. The balloon at first collapsed, then furiously expanded, then whirled round and round with horrible velocity, and finally, reeling and staggering like a drunken man, hurled me with great force over the rim of the car, and left me dangling, at a terrific height, with my head downward, and my face outwards, by a piece of slender cord about three feet in length, which hung accidentally through a crevice near the bottom of the wicker-work, and in which, as I fell, my left foot became most providentially entangled. It is impossible — utterly impossible — to form any adequate idea of the horror of my situation. I gasped convulsively for breath — a shudder resembling a fit of the ague agitated every nerve and muscle of my frame — I felt my eyes starting from their sockets — a horrible nausea overwhelmed me — and at length I fainted away.

How long I remained in this state it is impossible to say. It must, however, have been no inconsiderable time, for when I partially recovered the sense of existence, I found the day breaking, the balloon at a prodigious height over a wilderness of ocean, and not a trace of land to be discovered far and wide within the limits of the vast horizon. My sensations, however, upon thus recovering, were by no means so rife with agony as might have been anticipated. Indeed, there was much of incipient madness in the calm survey which I began to take of my situation. I drew up to my eyes each of my hands, one after the other, and wondered what occurrence could have given rise to the swelling of the veins, and the horrible blackness of the fingernails. I afterward carefully examined my head, shaking it repeatedly, and feeling it with minute attention, until I succeeded in satisfying myself that it was not, as I had more than half suspected, larger than my balloon. Then, in a knowing manner, I felt in both my breeches pockets, and, missing therefrom a set of tablets and a toothpick case, endeavored to account for their disappearance, and not being able to do so, felt inexpressibly chagrined. It now occurred to me that I suffered great uneasiness in the joint of my left ankle, and a dim consciousness of my situation began to glimmer through my mind. But, strange to say! I was neither astonished nor horror-stricken. If I felt any emotion at all, it was a kind of chuckling satisfaction at the cleverness I was about to display in extricating myself from this dilemma; and I never, for a moment, looked upon my ultimate safety as a question susceptible of doubt. For a few minutes I remained wrapped in the profoundest meditation. I have a distinct recollection of frequently compressing my lips, putting my forefinger to the side of my nose, and making use of other gesticulations and grimaces common to men who, at ease in their armchairs, meditate upon matters of intricacy or importance. Having, as I thought, sufficiently collected my ideas, I now, with great caution and deliberation, put my hands behind my back, and unfastened the large iron buckle which belonged to the waistband of my inexpressibles. This buckle had three teeth, which, being somewhat rusty, turned with great difficulty on their axis. I brought them, however, after some trouble, at right angles to the body of the buckle, and was glad to find them remain firm in that position. Holding the instrument thus obtained within my teeth, I now proceeded to untie the knot of my cravat. I had to rest several times before I could accomplish this manoeuvre, but it was at length accomplished. To one end of the cravat I then made fast the buckle, and the other end I tied, for greater security, tightly around my wrist. Drawing now my body upwards, with a prodigious exertion of muscular force, I succeeded, at the very first trial, in throwing the buckle over the car, and entangling it, as I had anticipated, in the circular rim of the wicker-work.

My body was now inclined towards the side of the car, at an angle of about forty-five degrees; but it must not be understood that I was therefore only forty-five degrees below the perpendicular. So far from it, I still lay nearly level with the plane of the horizon; for the change of situation which I had acquired, had forced the bottom of the car considerably outwards from my position, which was accordingly one of the most imminent and deadly peril. It should be remembered, however, that when I fell in the first instance, from the car, if I had fallen with my face turned toward the balloon, instead of turned outwardly from it, as it actually was; or if, in the second place, the cord by which I was suspended had chanced to hang over the upper edge, instead of through a crevice near the bottom of the car — I say it may be readily conceived that, in either of these supposed cases, I should have been unable to accomplish even as much as I had now accomplished, and the wonderful adventures of Hans Pfaall would have been utterly lost to posterity, I had therefore every reason to be grateful; although, in point of fact, I was still too stupid to be anything at all, and hung for, perhaps, a quarter of an hour in that extraordinary manner, without making the slightest farther exertion whatsoever, and in a singularly tranquil state of idiotic enjoyment. But this feeling did not fail to die rapidly away, and thereunto succeeded horror, and dismay, and a chilling sense of utter helplessness and ruin. In fact, the blood so long accumulating in the vessels of my head and throat, and which had hitherto buoyed up my spirits with madness and delirium, had now begun to retire within their proper channels, and the distinctness which was thus added to my perception of the danger, merely served to deprive me of the self-possession and courage to encounter it. But this weakness was, luckily for me, of no very long duration. In good time came to my rescue the spirit of despair, and, with frantic cries and struggles, I jerked my way bodily upwards, till at length, clutching with a vise-like grip the long-desired rim, I writhed my person over it, and fell headlong and shuddering within the car.

It was not until some time afterward that I recovered myself sufficiently to attend to the ordinary cares of the balloon. I then, however, examined it with attention, and found it, to my great relief, uninjured. My implements were all safe, and, fortunately, I had lost neither ballast nor provisions. Indeed, I had so well secured them in their places, that such an accident was entirely out of the question. Looking at my watch, I found it six o'clock. I was still rapidly ascending, and my barometer gave a present altitude of three and three-quarter miles. Immediately beneath me in the ocean, lay a small black object, slightly oblong in shape, seemingly about the size, and in every way bearing a great resemblance to one of those childish toys called a domino. Bringing my telescope to bear upon it, I plainly discerned it to be a British ninety four-gun ship, closehauled, and pitching heavily in the sea with her head to the W.S.W. Besides this ship, I saw nothing but the ocean and the sky, and the sun, which had long arisen.

It is now high time that I should explain to your Excellencies the object of my perilous voyage. Your Excellencies will bear in mind that distressed circumstances in Rotterdam had at length driven me to the resolution of committing suicide. It was not, however, that to life itself I had any, positive disgust, but that I was harassed beyond endurance by the adventitious miseries attending my situation. In this state of mind, wishing to live, yet wearied with life, the treatise at the stall of the bookseller opened a resource to my imagination. I then finally made up my mind. I determined to depart, yet live — to leave the world, yet continue to exist — in short, to drop enigmas, I resolved, let what would ensue, to force a passage, if I could, to the moon. Now, lest I should be supposed more of a madman than I actually am, I will detail, as well as I am able, the considerations which led me to believe that an achievement of this nature, although without doubt difficult, and incontestably full of danger, was not absolutely, to a bold spirit, beyond the confines of the possible.

The moon's actual distance from the earth was the first thing to be attended to. Now, the mean or average interval between the centres of the two planets is 59.9643 of the earth's equatorial radii, or only about 237,000 miles. I say the mean or average interval. But it must be borne in mind that the form of the moon's orbit being an ellipse of eccentricity amounting to no less than 0.05484 of the major semi-axis of the ellipse itself, and the earth's centre being situated in its focus, if I could, in any manner, contrive to meet the moon, as it were, in its perigee, the above mentioned distance would be materially diminished. But, to say nothing at present of this possibility, it was very certain that, at all events, from the 237,000 miles I would have to deduct the radius of the earth, say 4,000, and the radius of the moon, say 1080, in all 5,080, leaving an actual interval to be traversed, under average circumstances, of 231,920 miles. Now this, I reflected, was no very extraordinary distance. Travelling on land has been repeatedly accomplished at the rate of thirty miles per hour, and indeed a much greater speed may be anticipated. But even at this velocity, it would take me no more than 322 days to reach the surface of the moon. There were, however, many particulars inducing me to believe that my average rate of travelling might possibly very much exceed that of thirty miles per hour, and, as these considerations did not fail to make a deep impression upon my mind, I will mention them more fully hereafter.

The next point to be regarded was a matter of far greater importance. From indications afforded by the barometer, we find that, in ascensions from the surface of the earth we have, at the height of 1,000 feet, left below us about one-thirtieth of the entire mass of atmospheric air, that at 10,600 we have ascended through nearly one-third; and that at 18,000, which is not far from the elevation of Cotopaxi, we have surmounted one-half the material, or, at all events, one-half the ponderable, body of air incumbent upon our globe. It is also calculated that at an altitude not exceeding the hundredth part of the earth's diameter — that is, not exceeding eighty miles — the rarefaction would be so excessive that animal life could in no manner be sustained, and, moreover, that the most delicate means we possess of ascertaining the presence of the atmosphere would be inadequate to assure us of its existence. But I did not fail to perceive that these latter calculations are founded altogether on our experimental knowledge of the properties of air, and the mechanical laws regulating its dilation and compression, in what may be called, comparatively speaking, the immediate vicinity of the earth itself; and, at the same time, it is taken for granted that animal life is and must be essentially incapable of modification at any given unattainable distance from the surface. Now, all such reasoning and from such data must, of course, be simply analogical. The greatest height ever reached by man was that of 25,000 feet, attained in the aeronautic expedition of Messieurs Gay-Lussac and Biot. This is a moderate altitude, even when compared with the eighty miles in question; and I could not help thinking that the subject admitted room for doubt and great latitude for speculation.

But, in point of fact, an ascension being made to any given altitude, the ponderable quantity of air surmounted in any farther ascension is by no means in proportion to the additional height ascended (as may be plainly seen from what has been stated before), but in a ratio constantly decreasing. It is therefore evident that, ascend as high as we may, we cannot, literally speaking, arrive at a limit beyond which no atmosphere is to be found. It must exist, I argued; although it may exist in a state of infinite rarefaction.

On the other hand, I was aware that arguments have not been wanting to prove the existence of a real and definite limit to the atmosphere, beyond which there is absolutely no air whatsoever. But a circumstance which has been left out of view by those who contend for such a limit seemed to me, although no positive refutation of their creed, still a point worthy very serious investigation. On comparing the intervals between the successive arrivals of Encke's comet at its perihelion, after giving credit, in the most exact manner, for all the disturbances due to the attractions of the planets, it appears that the periods are gradually diminishing; that is to say, the major axis of the comet's ellipse is growing shorter, in a slow but perfectly regular decrease. Now, this is precisely what ought to be the case, if we suppose a resistance experienced from the comet from an extremely rare ethereal medium pervading the regions of its orbit. For it is evident that such a medium must, in retarding the comet's velocity, increase its centripetal, by weakening its centrifugal force. In other words, the sun's attraction would be constantly attaining greater power, and the comet would be drawn nearer at every revolution. Indeed, there is no other way of accounting for the variation in question. But again. The real diameter of the same comet's nebulosity is observed to contract rapidly as it approaches the sun, and dilate with equal rapidity in its departure towards its aphelion. Was I not justifiable in supposing with M. Valz, that this apparent condensation of volume has its origin in the compression of the same ethereal medium I have spoken of before, and which is only denser in proportion to its solar vicinity? The lenticular-shaped phenomenon, also called the zodiacal light, was a matter worthy of attention. This radiance, so apparent in the tropics, and which cannot be mistaken for any meteoric lustre, extends from the horizon obliquely upward, and follows generally the direction of the sun's equator. It appeared to me evidently in the nature of a rare atmosphere extending from the sun outward, beyond the orbit of Venus at least, and I believed indefinitely farther. [1] Indeed, this medium I could not suppose confined to the path of the comet's ellipse, or to the immediate neighborhood of the sun. It was easy, on the contrary, to imagine it pervading the entire regions of our planetary system, condensed into what we call atmosphere at the planets themselves, and perhaps at some of them modified by considerations, so to speak, purely geological. Having adopted this view of the subject, I had little further hesitation. Granting that on my passage I should meet with atmosphere essentially the same as at the surface of the earth, I conceived that, by means of the very ingenious apparatus of M. Grimm, I should readily be enabled to condense it in sufficient quantity for the purposes of respiration. This would remove the chief obstacle in a journey to the moon. I had indeed spent some money and great labor in adapting the apparatus to the object intended, and confidently looked forward to its successful application, if I could manage to complete the voyage within any reasonable period. This brings me back to the rate at which it might be possible to travel.

It is true that balloons, in the first stage of their ascensions from the earth, are known to rise with a velocity comparatively moderate. Now, the power of elevation lies altogether in the superior lightness of the gas in the balloon compared with the atmospheric air; and, at first sight, it does not appear probable that, as the balloon acquires altitude, and consequently arrives successively in atmospheric strata of densities rapidly diminishing — I say, it does not appear at all reasonable that, in this its progress upwards, the original velocity should be accelerated. On the other hand, I was not aware that, in any recorded ascension, a diminution was apparent in the absolute rate of ascent; although such should have been the case, if on account of nothing else, on account of the escape of gas through balloons ill-constructed, and varnished with no better material than the ordinary varnish. It seemed, therefore, that the effect of such escape was only sufficient to counterbalance the effect of some accelerating power. I now considered that, provided in my passage I found the medium I had imagined, and provided that it should prove to be actually and essentially what we denominate atmospheric air, it could make comparatively little difference at what extreme state of rarefaction I should discover it — that is to say, in regard to my power of ascending — for the gas in the balloon would not only be itself subject to rarefaction partially similar (in proportion to the occurrence of which, I could suffer an escape of so much as would be requisite to prevent explosion), but, being what it was, would, at all events, continue specifically lighter than any compound whatever of mere nitrogen and oxygen. In the meantime, the force of gravitation would be constantly diminishing, in proportion to the squares of the distances, and thus, with a velocity prodigiously accelerating, I should at length arrive in those distant regions where the force of the earth's attraction would be superseded by that of the moon. In accordance with these ideas, I did not think it worthwhile to encumber myself with more provisions than would be sufficient for a period of forty days.

There was still, however, another difficulty, which occasioned me some little disquietude. It has been observed, that, in balloon ascensions to any considerable height, besides the pain attending respiration, great uneasiness is experienced about the head and body, often accompanied with bleeding at the nose, and other symptoms of an alarming kind, and growing more and more inconvenient in proportion to the altitude attained. [2] This was a reflection of a nature somewhat startling. Was it not probable that these symptoms would increase indefinitely, or at least until terminated by death itself? I finally thought not. Their origin was to be looked for in the progressive removal of the customary atmospheric pressure upon the surface of the body, and consequent distention of the superficial blood-vessels — not in any positive disorganization of the animal system, as in the case of difficulty in breathing, where the atmospheric density is chemically insufficient for the due renovation of blood in a ventricle of the heart. Unless for default of this renovation, I could see no reason, therefore, why life could not be sustained even in a vacuum; for the expansion and compression of chest, commonly called breathing, is action purely muscular, and the cause, not the effect, of respiration. In a word, I conceived that, as the body should become habituated to the want of atmospheric pressure, the sensations of pain would gradually diminish — and to endure them while they continued, I relied with confidence upon the iron hardihood of my constitution.

Thus, may it please your Excellencies, I have detailed some, though by no means all, the considerations which led me to form the project of a lunar voyage. I shall now proceed to lay before you the result of an attempt so apparently audacious in conception, and, at all events, so utterly unparalleled in the annals of mankind.

Having attained the altitude before mentioned, that is to say three miles and three-quarters, I threw out from the car a quantity of feathers, and found that I still ascended with sufficient rapidity; there was, therefore, no necessity for discharging any ballast. I was glad of this, for I wished to retain with me as much weight as I could carry, for reasons which will be explained in the sequel. I as yet suffered no bodily inconvenience, breathing with great freedom, and feeling no pain whatever in the head. The cat was lying very demurely upon my coat, which I had taken off, and eyeing the pigeons with an air of nonchalance. These latter being tied by the leg, to prevent their escape, were busily employed in picking up some grains of rice scattered for them in the bottom of the car.

At twenty minutes past six o'clock, the barometer showed an elevation of 26,400 feet, or five miles to a fraction. The prospect seemed unbounded. Indeed, it is very easily calculated by means of spherical geometry, what a great extent of the earth's area I beheld. The convex surface of any segment of a sphere is, to the entire surface of the sphere itself, as the versed sine of the segment to the diameter of the sphere. Now, in my case, the versed sine — that is to say, the thickness of the segment beneath me — was about equal to my elevation, or the elevation of the point of sight above the surface. "As five miles, then, to eight thousand," would express the proportion of the earth's area seen by me. In other words, I beheld as much as a sixteen-hundredth part of the whole surface of the globe. The sea appeared unruffled as a mirror, although, by means of the spy-glass, I could perceive it to be in a state of violent agitation. The ship was no longer visible, having drifted away, apparently to the eastward. I now began to experience, at intervals, severe pain in the head, especially about the ears — still, however, breathing with tolerable freedom. The cat and pigeons seemed to suffer no inconvenience whatsoever.

At twenty minutes before seven, the balloon entered a long series of dense cloud, which put me to great trouble, by damaging my condensing apparatus and wetting me to the skin. This was, to be sure, a singular recontre, for I had not believed it possible that a cloud of this nature could be sustained at so great an elevation. I thought it best, however, to throw out two five-pound pieces of ballast, reserving still a weight of one hundred and sixty-five pounds. Upon so doing, I soon rose above the difficulty, and perceived immediately, that I had obtained a great increase in my rate of ascent. In a few seconds after my leaving the cloud, a flash of vivid lightning shot from one end of it to the other, and caused it to kindle up, throughout its vast extent, like a mass of ignited and glowing charcoal. This, it must be remembered, was in the broad light of day. No fancy may picture the sublimity which might have been exhibited by a similar phenomenon taking place amid the darkness of the night. Hell itself might have been found a fitting image. Even as it was, my hair stood on end, while I gazed afar down within the yawning abysses, letting imagination descend, as it were, and stalk about in the strange vaulted halls, and ruddy gulfs, and red ghastly chasms of the hideous and unfathomable fire. I had indeed made a narrow escape. Had the balloon remained a very short while longer within the cloud — that is to say — had not the inconvenience of getting wet, determined me to discharge the ballast, inevitable ruin would have been the consequence. Such perils, although little considered, are perhaps the greatest which must be encountered in balloons. I had by this time, however, attained too great an elevation to be any longer uneasy on this head.

I was now rising rapidly, and by seven o'clock the barometer indicated an altitude of no less than nine miles and a half. I began to find great difficulty in drawing my breath. My head, too, was excessively painful; and, having felt for some time a moisture about my cheeks, I at length discovered it to be blood, which was oozing quite fast from the drums of my ears. My eyes, also, gave me great uneasiness. Upon passing the hand over them they seemed to have protruded from their sockets in no inconsiderable degree; and all objects in the car, and even the balloon itself, appeared distorted to my vision. These symptoms were more than I had expected, and occasioned me some alarm. At this juncture, very imprudently, and without consideration, I threw out from the car three five-pound pieces of ballast. The accelerated rate of ascent thus obtained, carried me too rapidly, and without sufficient gradation, into a highly rarefied stratum of the atmosphere, and the result had nearly proved fatal to my expedition and to myself. I was suddenly seized with a spasm which lasted for more than five minutes, and even when this, in a measure, ceased, I could catch my breath only at long intervals, and in a gasping manner — bleeding all the while copiously at the nose and ears, and even slightly at the eyes.

The pigeons appeared distressed in the extreme, and struggled to escape; while the cat mewed piteously, and, with her tongue hanging out of her mouth, staggered to and fro in the car as if under the influence of poison. I now too late discovered the great rashness of which I had been guilty in discharging the ballast, and my agitation was excessive. I anticipated nothing less than death, and death in a few minutes. The physical suffering I underwent contributed also to render me nearly incapable of making any exertion for the preservation of my life. I had, indeed, little power of reflection left, and the violence of the pain in my head seemed to be greatly on the increase. Thus I found that my senses would shortly give way altogether, and I had already clutched one of the valve ropes with the view of attempting a descent, when the recollection of the trick I had played the three creditors, and the possible consequences to myself, should I return, operated to deter me for the moment. I lay down in the bottom of the car, and endeavored to collect my faculties. In this I so far succeeded as to determine upon the experiment of losing blood. Having no lancet, however, I was constrained to perform the operation in the best manner I was able, and finally succeeded in opening a vein in my right arm, with the blade of my penknife. The blood had hardly commenced flowing when I experienced a sensible relief, and by the time I had lost about half a moderate basin full, most of the worst symptoms had abandoned me entirely. I nevertheless did not think it expedient to attempt getting on my feet immediately; but, having tied up my arm as well as I could, I lay still for about a quarter of an hour. At the end of this time I arose, and found myself freer from absolute pain of any kind than I had been during the last hour and a quarter of my ascension. The difficulty of breathing, however, was diminished in a very slight degree, and I found that it would soon be positively necessary to make use of my condenser. In the meantime, looking toward the cat, who was again snugly stowed away upon my coat, I discovered to my infinite surprise, that she had taken the opportunity of my indisposition to bring into light a litter of three little kittens. This was an addition to the number of passengers on my part altogether unexpected; but I was pleased at the occurrence. It would afford me a chance of bringing to a kind of test the truth of a surmise, which, more than anything else, had influenced me in attempting this ascension. I had imagined that the habitual endurance of the atmospheric pressure at the surface of the earth was the cause, or nearly so, of the pain attending animal existence at a distance above the surface. Should the kittens be found to suffer uneasiness in an equal degree with their mother, I must consider my theory in fault, but a failure to do so I should look upon as a strong confirmation of my idea.

By eight o'clock I had actually attained an elevation of seventeen miles above the surface of the earth. Thus it seemed to me evident that my rate of ascent was not only on the increase, but that the progression would have been apparent in a slight degree even had I not discharged the ballast which I did. The pains in my head and ears returned, at intervals, with violence, and I still continued to bleed occasionally at the nose; but, upon the whole, I suffered much less than might have been expected. I breathed, however, at every moment, with more and more difficulty, and each inhalation was attended with a troublesome spasmodic action of the chest. I now unpacked the condensing apparatus, and got it ready for immediate use.

The view of the earth, at this period of my ascension, was beautiful indeed. To the westward, the northward, and the southward, as far as I could see, lay a boundless sheet of apparently unruffled ocean, which every moment gained a deeper and a deeper tint of blue and began already to assume a slight appearance of convexity. At a vast distance to the eastward, although perfectly discernible, extended the islands of Great Britain, the entire Atlantic coasts of France and Spain, with a small portion of the northern part of the continent of Africa. Of individual edifices not a trace could be discovered, and the proudest cities of mankind had utterly faded away from the face of the earth. From the rock of Gibraltar, now dwindled into a dim speck, the dark Mediterranean sea, dotted with shining islands as the heaven is dotted with stars, spread itself out to the eastward as far as my vision extended, until its entire mass of waters seemed at length to tumble headlong over the abyss of the horizon, and I found myself listening on tiptoe for the echoes of the mighty cataract. Overhead, the sky was of a jetty black, and the stars were brilliantly visible.

The pigeons about this time seeming to undergo much suffering, I determined upon giving them their liberty. I first untied one of them, a beautiful gray-mottled pigeon, and placed him upon the rim of the wicker-work. He appeared extremely uneasy, looking anxiously around him, fluttering his wings, and making a loud cooing noise, but could not be persuaded to trust himself from off the car. I took him up at last, and threw him to about half a dozen yards from the balloon. He made, however, no attempt to descend as I had expected, but struggled with great vehemence to get back, uttering at the same time very shrill and piercing cries. He at length succeeded in regaining his former station on the rim, but had hardly done so when his head dropped upon his breast, and be fell dead within the car. The other one did not prove so unfortunate. To prevent his following the example of his companion, and accomplishing a return, I threw him downward with all my force, and was pleased to find him continue his descent, with great velocity, making use of his wings with ease, and in a perfectly natural manner. In a very short time he was out of sight, and I have no doubt he reached home in safety. Puss, who seemed in a great measure recovered from her illness, now made a hearty meal of the dead bird and then went to sleep with much apparent satisfaction. Her kittens were quite lively, and so far evinced not the slightest sign of any uneasiness whatever.

At a quarter-past eight, being no longer able to draw breath without the most intolerable pain, I proceeded forthwith to adjust around the car the apparatus belonging to the condenser. This apparatus will require some little explanation, and your Excellencies will please to bear in mind that my object, in the first place, was to surround myself and cat entirely with a barricade against the highly rarefied atmosphere in which I was existing, with the intention of introducing within this barricade, by means of my condenser, a quantity of this same atmosphere sufficiently condensed for the purposes of respiration. With this object in view I had prepared a very strong perfectly air-tight, but flexible gum-elastic bag. In this bag, which was of sufficient dimensions, the entire car was in a manner placed. That is to say, it (the bag) was drawn over the whole bottom of the car, up its sides, and so on, along the outside of the ropes, to the upper rim or hoop where the net-work is attached. Having pulled the bag up in this way, and formed a complete enclosure on all sides, and at bottom, it was now necessary to fasten up its top or mouth, by passing its material over the hoop of the net-work — in other words, between the net-work and the hoop. But if the net-work were separated from the hoop to admit this passage, what was to sustain the car in the meantime? Now the net-work was not permanently fastened to the hoop, but attached by a series of running loops or nooses. I therefore undid only a few of these loops at one time, leaving the car suspended by the remainder. Having thus inserted a portion of the cloth forming the upper part of the bag, I refastened the loops — not to the hoop, for that would have been impossible, since the cloth now intervened — but to a series of large buttons, affixed to the cloth itself, about three feet below the mouth of the bag, the intervals between the buttons having been made to correspond to the intervals between the loops. This done, a few more of the loops were unfastened from the rim, a farther portion of the cloth introduced, and the disengaged loops then connected with their proper buttons. In this way it was possible to insert the whole upper part of the bag between the net-work and the hoop. It is evident that the hoop would now drop down within the car, while the whole weight of the car itself, with all its contents, would be held up merely by the strength of the buttons. This, at first sight, would seem an inadequate dependence; but it was by no means so, for the buttons were not only very strong in themselves, but so close together that a very slight portion of the whole weight was supported by any one of them. Indeed, had the car and contents been three times heavier than they were, I should not have been at all uneasy. I now raised up the hoop again within the covering of gum-elastic, and propped it at nearly its former height by means of three light poles prepared for the occasion. This was done, of course, to keep the bag distended at the top, and to preserve the lower part of the net-work in its proper situation. All that now remained was to fasten up the mouth of the enclosure; and this was readily accomplished by gathering the folds of the material together, and twisting them up very tightly on the inside by means of a kind of stationary tourniquet.

In the sides of the covering thus adjusted round the car, had been inserted three circular panes of thick but clear glass, through which I could see without difficulty around me in every horizontal direction. In that portion of the cloth forming the bottom, was likewise, a fourth window, of the same kind, and corresponding with a small aperture in the floor of the car itself. This enabled me to see perpendicularly down, but having found it impossible to place any similar contrivance overhead, on account of the peculiar manner of closing up the opening there, and the consequent wrinkles in the cloth, I could expect to see no objects situated directly in my zenith. This, of course, was a matter of little consequence; for had I even been able to place a window at top, the balloon itself would have prevented my making any use of it.

About a foot below one of the side windows was a circular opening, eight inches in diameter, and fitted with a brass rim adapted in its inner edge to the windings of a screw. In this rim was screwed the large tube of the condenser, the body of the machine being, of course, within the chamber of gum-elastic. Through this tube a quantity of the rare atmosphere circumjacent being drawn by means of a vacuum created in the body of the machine, was thence discharged, in a state of condensation, to mingle with the thin air already in the chamber. This operation being repeated several times, at length filled the chamber with atmosphere proper for all the purposes of respiration. But in so confined a space it would, in a short time, necessarily become foul, and unfit for use from frequent contact with the lungs. It was then ejected by a small valve at the bottom of the car — the dense air readily sinking into the thinner atmosphere below. To avoid the inconvenience of making a total vacuum at any moment within the chamber, this purification was never accomplished all at once, but in a gradual manner — the valve being opened only for a few seconds, then closed again, until one or two strokes from the pump of the condenser had supplied the place of the atmosphere ejected. For the sake of experiment I had put the cat and kittens in a small basket, and suspended it outside the car to a button at the bottom, close by the valve, through which I could feed them at any moment when necessary. I did this at some little risk, and before closing the mouth of the chamber, by reaching under the car with one of the poles before mentioned to which a hook had been attached.

By the time I had fully completed these arrangements and filled the chamber as explained, it wanted only ten minutes of nine o'clock. During the whole period of my being thus employed, I endured the most terrible distress from difficulty of respiration, and bitterly did I repent the negligence or rather fool-hardiness, of which I had been guilty, of putting off to the last moment a matter of so much importance. But having at length accomplished it, I soon began to reap the benefit of my invention. Once again I breathed with perfect freedom and ease — and indeed why should I not? I was also agreeably surprised to find myself, in a great measure, relieved from the violent pains which had hitherto tormented me. A slight headache, accompanied with a sensation of fullness or distension about the wrists, the ankles, and the throat, was nearly all of which I had now to complain. Thus it seemed evident that a greater part of the uneasiness attending the removal of atmospheric pressure had actually worn off, as I had expected, and that much of the pain endured for the last two hours should have been attributed altogether to the effects of a deficient respiration.

At twenty minutes before nine o'clock — that is to say, a short time prior to my closing up the mouth of the chamber, the mercury attained its limit, or ran down, in the barometer, which, as I mentioned before, was one of an extended construction. It then indicated an altitude on my part of 132,000 feet, or five-and-twenty miles, and I consequently surveyed at that time an extent of the earth's area amounting to no less than the three hundred-and-twentieth part of its entire superficies. At nine o'clock I had again lost sight of land to the eastward, but not before I became aware that the balloon was drifting rapidly to the N.N.W. The convexity of the ocean beneath me was very evident indeed, although my view was often interrupted by the masses of cloud which floated to and fro. I observed now that even the lightest vapors never rose to more than ten miles above the level of the sea. At half past nine I tried the experiment of throwing out a handful of feathers through the valve. They did not float as I had expected; but dropped down perpendicularly, like a bullet, en masse, and with the greatest velocity — being out of sight in a very few seconds. I did not at first know what to make of this extraordinary phenomenon; not being able to believe that my rate of ascent had, of a sudden, met with so prodigious an acceleration. But it soon occurred to me that the atmosphere was now far too rare to sustain even the feathers; that they actually fell, as they appeared to do, with great rapidity; and that I had been surprised by the united velocities of their descent and my own elevation.

By ten o'clock I found that I had very little to occupy my immediate attention. Affairs went swimmingly, and I believed the balloon to be going upward with a speed increasing momently although I had no longer any means of ascertaining the progression of the increase. I suffered no pain or uneasiness of any kind, and enjoyed better spirits than I had at any period since my departure from

Rotterdam, busying myself now in examining the state of my various apparatus, and now in regenerating the atmosphere within the chamber. This latter point I determined to attend to at regular intervals of forty minutes, more on account of the preservation of my health, than from so frequent a renovation being absolutely necessary. In the meanwhile I could not help making anticipations. Fancy revelled in the wild and dreamy regions of the moon. Imagination, feeling herself for once unshackled, roamed at will among the ever-changing wonders of a shadowy and unstable land. Now there were boary and time-honored forests, and craggy precipices, and waterfalls tumbling with a loud noise into abysses without a bottom. Then I came suddenly into still noonday solitudes, where no wind of heaven ever intruded, and where vast meadows of poppies, and slender, lily-looking flowers spread themselves out a weary distance, all silent and motionless forever. Then again I journeyed far down away into another country where it was all one dim and vague lake, with a boundary line of clouds. And out of this melancholy water arose a forest of tall eastern trees, like a wilderness of dreams. And I have in mind that the shadows of the trees which fell upon the lake remained not on the surface where they fell, but sunk slowly and steadily down, and commingled with the waves, while from the trunks of the trees other shadows were continually coming out, and taking the place of their brothers thus entombed. "This then," I said thoughtfully, "is the very reason why the waters of this lake grow blacker with age, and more melancholy as the hours run on." But fancies such as these were not the sole possessors of my brain. Horrors of a nature most stern and most appalling would too frequently obtrude themselves upon my mind, and shake the innermost depths of my soul with the bare supposition of their possibility. Yet I would not suffer my thoughts for any length of time to dwell upon these latter speculations, rightly judging the real and palpable dangers of the voyage sufficient for my undivided attention.

At five o'clock, P.M., being engaged in regenerating the atmosphere within the chamber, I took that opportunity of observing the cat and kittens through the valve. The cat herself appeared to suffer again very much, and I had no hesitation in attributing her uneasiness chiefly to a difficulty in breathing; but my experiment with the kittens had resulted very strangely. I had expected, of course, to see them betray a sense of pain, although in a less degree than their mother, and this would have been sufficient to confirm my opinion concerning the habitual endurance of atmospheric pressure. But I was not prepared to find them, upon close examination, evidently enjoying a high degree of health, breathing with the greatest ease and perfect regularity, and evincing not the slightest sign of any uneasiness whatever. I could only account for all this by extending my theory, and supposing that the highly rarefied atmosphere around might perhaps not be, as I had taken for granted, chemically insufficient for the purposes of life, and that a person born in such a medium might, possibly, be unaware of any inconvenience attending its inhalation, while, upon removal to the denser strata near the earth, he might endure tortures of a similar nature to those I had so lately experienced. It has since been to me a matter of deep regret that an awkward accident, at this time, occasioned me the loss of my little family of cats, and deprived me of the insight into this matter which a continued experiment might have afforded. In passing my hand through the valve, with a cup of water for the old puss, the sleeves of my shirt became entangled in the loop which sustained the basket, and thus, in a moment, loosened it from the bottom. Had the whole actually vanished into air, it could not have shot from my sight in a more abrupt and instantaneous manner. Positively, there could not have intervened the tenth part of a second between the disengagement of the basket and its absolute and total disappearance with all that it contained. My good wishes followed it to the earth, but of course, I had no hope that either cat or kittens would ever live to tell the tale of their misfortune.

At six o'clock, I perceived a great portion of the earth's visible area to the eastward involved in thick shadow, which continued to advance with great rapidity, until, at five minutes before seven, the whole surface in view was enveloped in the darkness of night. It was not, however, until long after this time that the rays of the setting sun ceased to illumine the balloon; and this circumstance, although of course fully anticipated, did not fail to give me an infinite deal of pleasure. It was evident that, in the morning, I should behold the rising luminary many hours at least before the citizens of Rotterdam, in spite of their situation so much farther to the eastward, and thus, day after day, in proportion to the height ascended, would I enjoy the light of the sun for a longer and a longer period. I now determined to keep a journal of my passage, reckoning the days from one to twenty-four hours continuously, without taking into consideration the intervals of darkness.

At ten o'clock, feeling sleepy, I determined to lie down for the rest of the night; but here a difficulty presented itself, which, obvious as it may appear, had escaped my attention up to the very moment of which I am now speaking. If I went to sleep as I proposed, how could the atmosphere in the chamber be regenerated in the interim? To breathe it for more than an hour, at the farthest, would be a matter of impossibility, or, if even this term could be extended to an hour and a quarter, the most ruinous consequences might ensue. The consideration of this dilemma gave me no little disquietude; and it will hardly be believed, that, after the dangers I had undergone, I should look upon this business in so serious a light, as to give up all hope of accomplishing my ultimate design, and finally make up my mind to the necessity of a descent. But this hesitation was only momentary. I reflected that man is the veriest slave of custom, and that many points in the routine of his existence are deemed essentially important, which are only so at all by his having rendered them habitual. It was very certain that I could not do without sleep; but I might easily bring myself to feel no inconvenience from being awakened at intervals of an hour during the whole period of my repose. It would require but five minutes at most to regenerate the atmosphere in the fullest manner, and the only real difficulty was to contrive a method of arousing myself at the proper moment for so doing. But this was a question which, I am willing to confess, occasioned me no little trouble in its solution. To be sure, I had heard of the student who, to prevent his falling asleep over his books, held in one hand a ball of copper, the din of whose descent into a basin of the same metal on the floor beside his chair, served effectually to startle him up, if, at any moment, he should be overcome with drowsiness. My own case, however, was very different indeed, and left me no room for any similar idea; for I did not wish to keep awake, but to be aroused from slumber at regular intervals of time. I at length hit upon the following expedient, which, simple as it may seem, was hailed by me, at the moment of discovery, as an invention fully equal to that of the telescope, the steam-engine, or the art of printing itself.

It is necessary to premise, that the balloon, at the elevation now attained, continued its course upward with an even and undeviating ascent, and the car consequently followed with a steadiness so perfect that it would have been impossible to detect in it the slightest vacillation whatever. This circumstance favored me greatly in the project I now determined to adopt. My supply of water had been put on board in kegs containing five gallons each, and ranged very securely around the interior of the car. I unfastened one of these, and taking two ropes tied them tightly across the rim of the wicker-work from one side to the other; placing them about a foot apart and parallel so as to form a kind of shelf, upon which I placed the keg, and steadied it in a horizontal position. About eight inches immediately below these ropes, and four feet from the bottom of the car I fastened another shelf — but made of thin plank, being the only similar piece of wood I had. Upon this latter shelf, and exactly beneath one of the rims of the keg, a small earthern pitcher was deposited. I now bored a hole in the end of the keg over the pitcher, and fitted in a plug of soft wood, but in a tapering or conical shape. This plug I pushed in or pulled out, as might happen, until, after a few experiments, it arrived at that exact degree of tightness, at which the water, oozing from the hole, and falling into the pitcher below, would fill the latter to the brim in the period of sixty minutes. This, of course, was a matter briefly and easily ascertained, by noticing the proportion of the pitcher filled in any given time. Having arranged all this, the rest of the plan is obvious. My bed was so contrived upon the floor of the car, as to bring my head, in lying down, immediately below the mouth of the pitcher. It was evident, that, at the expiration of an hour, the pitcher, getting full, would be forced to run over, and to run over at the mouth, which was somewhat lower than the rim. It was also evident, that the water thus falling from a height of more than four feet, could not do otherwise than fall upon my face, and that the sure consequences would be, to waken me up instantaneously, even from the soundest slumber in the world.

It was fully eleven by the time I had completed these arrangements, and I immediately betook myself to bed, with full confidence in the efficiency of my invention. Nor in this matter was I disappointed. Punctually every sixty minutes was I aroused by my trusty chronometer, when, having emptied the pitcher into the bung-hole of the keg, and performed the duties of the condenser, I retired again to bed. These regular interruptions to my slumber caused me even less discomfort than I had anticipated; and when I finally arose for the day, it was seven o'clock, and the sun had attained many degrees above the line of my horizon.

April 3d. I found the balloon at an immense height indeed, and the earth's apparent convexity increased in a material degree. Below me in the ocean lay a cluster of black specks, which undoubtedly were islands. Far away to the northward I perceived a thin, white, and exceedingly brilliant line, or streak, on the edge of the horizon, and I had no hesitation in supposing it to be the southern disk of the ices of the Polar Sea. My curiosity was greatly excited, for I had hopes of passing on much farther to the north, and might possibly, at some period, find myself placed directly above the Pole itself. I now lamented that my great elevation would, in this case, prevent my taking as accurate a survey as I could wish. Much, however, might be ascertained. Nothing else of an extraordinary nature occurred during the day. My apparatus all continued in good order, and the balloon still ascended without any perceptible vacillation. The cold was intense, and obliged me to wrap up closely in an overcoat. When darkness came over the earth, I betook myself to bed, although it was for many hours afterward broad daylight all around my immediate situation. The water-clock was punctual in its duty, and I slept until next morning soundly, with the exception of the periodical interruption.

April 4th. Arose in good health and spirits, and was astonished at the singular change which had taken place in the appearance of the sea. It had lost, in a great measure, the deep tint of blue it had hitherto worn, being now of a grayish-white, and of a lustre dazzling to the eye. The islands were no longer visible; whether they had passed down the horizon to the southeast, or whether my increasing elevation had left them out of sight, it is impossible to say. I was inclined, however, to the latter opinion. The rim of ice to the northward was growing more and more apparent. Cold by no means so intense. Nothing of importance occurred, and I passed the day in reading, having taken care to supply myself with books.

April 5th. Beheld the singular phenomenon of the sun rising while nearly the whole visible surface of the earth continued to be involved in darkness. In time, however, the light spread itself over all, and I again saw the line of ice to the northward. It was now very distinct, and appeared of a much darker hue than the waters of the ocean. I was evidently approaching it, and with great rapidity. Fancied I could again distinguish a strip of land to the eastward, and one also to the westward, but could not be certain. Weather moderate. Nothing of any consequence happened during the day. Went early to bed.

April 6th. Was surprised at finding the rim of ice at a very moderate distance, and an immense field of the same material stretching away off to the horizon in the north. It was evident that if the balloon held its present course, it would soon arrive above the Frozen Ocean, and I had now little doubt of ultimately seeing the Pole. During the whole of the day I continued to near the ice. Toward night the limits of my horizon very suddenly and materially increased, owing undoubtedly to the earth's form being that of an oblate spheroid, and my arriving above the flattened regions in the vicinity of the Arctic circle. When darkness at length overtook me, I went to bed in great anxiety, fearing to pass over the object of so much curiosity when I should have no opportunity of observing it.

April 7th. Arose early, and, to my great joy, at length beheld what there could be no hesitation in supposing the northern Pole itself. It was there, beyond a doubt, and immediately beneath my feet; but, alas! I had now ascended to so vast a distance, that nothing could with accuracy be discerned. Indeed, to judge from the progression of the numbers indicating my various altitudes, respectively, at different periods, between six A.M. on the second of April, and twenty minutes before nine A.M. of the same day (at which time the barometer ran down), it might be fairly inferred that the balloon had now, at four o'clock in the morning of April the seventh, reached a height of not less, certainly, than 7,254 miles above the surface of the sea. This elevation may appear immense, but the estimate upon which it is calculated gave a result in all probability far inferior to the truth. At all events I undoubtedly beheld the whole of the earth's major diameter; the entire northern hemisphere lay beneath me like a chart orthographically projected: and the great circle of the equator itself formed the boundary line of my horizon. Your Excellencies may, however, readily imagine that the confined regions hitherto unexplored within the limits of the Arctic circle, although situated directly beneath me, and therefore seen without any appearance of being foreshortened, were still, in themselves, comparatively too diminutive, and at too great a distance from the point of sight, to admit of any very accurate examination. Nevertheless, what could be seen was of a nature singular and exciting. Northwardly from that huge rim before mentioned, and which, with slight qualification, may be called the limit of human discovery in these regions, one unbroken, or nearly unbroken, sheet of ice continues to extend. In the first few degrees of this its progress, its surface is very sensibly flattened, farther on depressed into a plane, and finally, becoming not a little concave, it terminates, at the Pole itself, in a circular centre, sharply defined, whose apparent diameter subtended at the balloon an angle of about sixty-five seconds, and whose dusky hue, varying in intensity, was, at all times, darker than any other spot upon the visible hemisphere, and occasionally deepened into the most absolute and impenetrable blackness. Farther than this, little could be ascertained. By twelve o'clock the circular centre had materially decreased in circumference, and by seven P.M. I lost sight of it entirely; the balloon passing over the western limb of the ice, and floating away rapidly in the direction of the equator.

April 8th. Found a sensible diminution in the earth's apparent diameter, besides a material alteration in its general color and appearance. The whole visible area partook in different degrees of a tint of pale yellow, and in some portions had acquired a brilliancy even painful to the eye. My view downward was also considerably impeded by the dense atmosphere in the vicinity of the surface being loaded with clouds, between whose masses I could only now and then obtain a glimpse of the earth itself. This difficulty of direct vision had troubled me more or less for the last forty-eight hours; but my present enormous elevation brought closer together, as it were, the floating bodies of vapor, and the inconvenience became, of course, more and more palpable in proportion to my ascent. Nevertheless, I could easily perceive that the balloon now hovered above the range of great lakes in the continent of North America, and was holding a course, due south, which would bring me to the tropics. This circumstance did not fail to give me the most heartful satisfaction, and I hailed it as a happy omen of ultimate success. Indeed, the direction I had hitherto taken, had filled me with uneasiness; for it was evident that, had I continued it much longer, there would have been no possibility of my arriving at the moon at all, whose orbit is inclined to the ecliptic at only the small angle of 5 degrees 8' 48".

April 9th. To-day the earth's diameter was greatly diminished, and the color of the surface assumed hourly a deeper tint of yellow. The balloon kept steadily on her course to the southward, and arrived, at nine P.M., over the northern edge of the Mexican Gulf.

April 10th. I was suddenly aroused from slumber, about five o'clock this morning, by a loud, crackling, and terrific sound, for which I could in no manner account. It was of very brief duration, but, while it lasted resembled nothing in the world of which I had any previous experience. It is needless to say that I became excessively alarmed, having, in the first instance, attributed the noise to the bursting of the balloon. I examined all my apparatus, however, with great attention, and could discover nothing out of order. Spent a great part of the day in meditating upon an occurrence so extraordinary, but could find no means whatever of accounting for it. Went to bed dissatisfied, and in a state of great anxiety and agitation.

April 11th. Found a startling diminution in the apparent diameter of the earth, and a considerable increase, now observable for the first time, in that of the moon itself, which wanted only a few days of being full. It now required long and excessive labor to condense within the chamber sufficient atmospheric air for the sustenance of life.

April 12th. A singular alteration took place in regard to the direction of the balloon, and although fully anticipated, afforded me the most unequivocal delight. Having reached, in its former course, about the twentieth parallel of southern latitude, it turned off suddenly, at an acute angle, to the eastward, and thus proceeded throughout the day, keeping nearly, if not altogether, in the exact plane of the lunar elipse. What was worthy of remark, a very perceptible vacillation in the car was a consequence of this change of route — a vacillation which prevailed, in a more or less degree, for a period of many hours.

April 13th. Was again very much alarmed by a repetition of the loud, crackling noise which terrified me on the tenth. Thought long upon the subject, but was unable to form any satisfactory conclusion. Great decrease in the earth's apparent diameter, which now subtended from the balloon an angle of very little more than twenty-five degrees. The moon could not be seen at all, being nearly in my zenith. I still continued in the plane of the elipse, but made little progress to the eastward.

April 14th. Extremely rapid decrease in the diameter of the earth. Today I became strongly impressed with the idea, that the balloon was now actually running up the line of apsides to the point of perigee — in other words, holding the direct course which would bring it immediately to the moon in that part of its orbit the nearest to the earth. The moon itself was directly overhead, and consequently hidden from my view. Great and long-continued labor necessary for the condensation of the atmosphere.

April 15th. Not even the outlines of continents and seas could now be traced upon the earth with anything approaching distinctness. About twelve o'clock I became aware, for the third time, of that appalling sound which had so astonished me before. It now, however, continued for some moments, and gathered intensity as it continued. At length, while, stupefied and terror-stricken, I stood in expectation of I knew not what hideous destruction, the car vibrated with excessive violence, and a gigantic and flaming mass of some material which I could not distinguish, came with a voice of a thousand thunders, roaring and booming by the balloon. When my fears and astonishment had in some degree subsided, I had little difficulty in supposing it to be some mighty volcanic fragment ejected from that world to which I was so rapidly approaching, and, in all probability, one of that singular class of substances occasionally picked up on the earth, and termed meteoric stones for want of a better appellation.

April 16th. To-day, looking upward as well as I could, through each of the side windows alternately, I beheld, to my great delight, a very small portion of the moon's disk protruding, as it were, on all sides beyond the huge circumference of the balloon. My agitation was extreme;

for I had now little doubt of soon reaching the end of my perilous voyage. Indeed, the labor now required by the condenser had increased to a most oppressive degree, and allowed me scarcely any respite from exertion. sleep was a matter nearly out of the question. I became quite ill, and my frame trembled with exhaustion. It was impossible that human nature could endure this state of intense suffering much longer. During the now brief interval of darkness a meteoric stone again passed in my vicinity, and the frequency of these phenomena began to occasion me much apprehension.

April 17th. This morning proved an epoch in my voyage. It will be remembered that, on the thirteenth, the earth subtended an angular breadth of twenty-five degrees. On the fourteenth this had greatly diminished; on the fifteenth a still more remarkable decrease was observable; and, on retiring on the night of the sixteenth, I had noticed an angle of no more than about seven degrees and fifteen minutes. What, therefore, must have been my amazement, on awakening from a brief and disturbed slumber, on the morning of this day, the seventeenth, at finding the surface beneath me so suddenly and wonderfully augmented in volume, as to subtend no less than thirty-nine degrees in apparent angular diameter! I was thunderstruck! No words can give any adequate idea of the extreme, the absolute horror and astonishment, with which I was seized possessed, and altogether overwhelmed. My knees tottered beneath me — my teeth chattered — my hair started up on end. "The balloon, then, had actually burst!" These were the first tumultuous ideas that hurried through my mind: "The balloon had positively burst! — I was falling — falling with the most impetuous, the most unparalleled velocity! To judge by the immense distance already so quickly passed over, it could not be more than ten minutes, at the farthest, before I should meet the surface of the earth, and be hurled into annihilation!" But at length reflection came to my relief. I paused; I considered; and I began to doubt. The matter was impossible. I could not in any reason have so rapidly come down. Besides, although I was evidently approaching the surface below me, it was with a speed by no means commensurate with the velocity I had at first so horribly conceived. This consideration served to calm the perturbation of my mind, and I finally succeeded in regarding the phenomenon in its proper point of view. In fact, amazement must have fairly deprived me of my senses, when I could not see the vast difference, in appearance, between the surface below me, and the surface of my mother earth. The latter was indeed over my head, and completely hidden by the balloon, while the moon — the moon itself in all its glory — lay beneath me, and at my feet.

The stupor and surprise produced in my mind by this extraordinary change in the posture of affairs was perhaps, after all, that part of the adventure least susceptible of explanation. For the bouleversement in itself was not only natural and inevitable, but had been long actually anticipated as a circumstance to be expected whenever I should arrive at that exact point of my voyage where the attraction of the planet should be superseded by the attraction of the satellite — or, more precisely, where the gravitation of the balloon toward the earth should be less powerful than its gravitation toward the moon. To be sure I arose from a sound slumber, with all my senses in confusion, to the contemplation of a very startling phenomenon, and one which, although expected, was not expected at the moment. The revolution itself must, of course, have taken place in an easy and gradual manner, and it is by no means clear that, had I even been awake at the time of the occurrence, I should have been made aware of it by any internal evidence of an inversion — that is to say, by any inconvenience or disarrangement, either about my person or about my apparatus.

It is almost needless to say that, upon coming to a due sense of my situation, and emerging from the terror which had absorbed every faculty of my soul, my attention was, in the first place, wholly directed to the contemplation of the general physical appearance of the moon. It lay beneath me like a chart — and although I judged it to be still at no inconsiderable distance, the indentures of its surface were defined to my vision with a most striking and altogether unaccountable distinctness. The entire absence of ocean or sea, and indeed of any lake or river, or body of water whatsoever, struck me, at first glance, as the most extraordinary feature in its geological condition. Yet, strange to say, I beheld vast level regions of a character decidedly alluvial, although by far the greater portion of the hemisphere in sight was covered with innumerable volcanic mountains, conical in shape, and having more the appearance of artificial than of natural protuberance. The highest among them does not exceed three and three-quarter miles in perpendicular elevation; but a map of the volcanic districts of the Campi Phlegraei would afford to your Excellencies a better idea of their general surface than any unworthy description I might think proper to attempt. The greater part of them were in a state of evident eruption, and gave me fearfully to understand their fury and their power, by the repeated thunders of the miscalled meteoric stones, which now rushed upward by the balloon with a frequency more and more appalling.

April 18th. To-day I found an enormous increase in the moon's apparent bulk — and the evidently accelerated velocity of my descent began to fill me with alarm. It will be remembered, that, in the earliest stage of my speculations upon the possibility of a passage to the moon, the existence, in its vicinity, of an atmosphere, dense in proportion to the bulk of the planet, had entered largely into my calculations; this too in spite of many theories to the contrary, and, it may be added, in spite of a general disbelief in the existence of any lunar atmosphere at all. But, in addition to what I have already urged in regard to Encke's comet and the zodiacal light, I had been strengthened in my opinion by certain observations of Mr. Schroeter, of Lilienthal. He observed the moon when two days and a half old, in the evening soon after sunset, before the dark part was visible, and continued to watch it until it became visible. The two cusps appeared tapering in a very sharp faint prolongation, each exhibiting its farthest extremity faintly illuminated by the solar rays, before any part of the dark hemisphere was visible. Soon afterward, the whole dark limb became illuminated. This prolongation of the cusps beyond the semicircle, I thought, must have arisen from the refraction of the sun's rays by the moon's atmosphere. I computed, also, the height of the atmosphere (which could refract light enough into its dark hemisphere to produce a twilight more luminous than the light reflected from the earth when the moon is about 32 degrees from the new) to be 1,356 Paris feet; in this view, I supposed the greatest height capable of refracting the solar ray, to be 5,376 feet. My ideas on this topic had also received confirmation by a passage in the eighty-second volume of the Philosophical Transactions, in which it is stated that at an occultation of Jupiter's satellites, the third disappeared after having been about 1" or 2" of time indistinct, and the fourth became indiscernible near the limb. [3]

Cassini frequently observed Saturn, Jupiter, and the fixed stars, when approaching the moon to occultation, to have their circular figure changed into an oval one; and, in other occultations, he found no alteration of figure at all. Hence it might be supposed, that at some times and not at others, there is a dense matter encompassing the moon wherein the rays of the stars are refracted.

Upon the resistance or, more properly, upon the support of an atmosphere, existing in the state of density imagined, I had, of course, entirely depended for the safety of my ultimate descent. Should I then, after all, prove to have been mistaken, I had in consequence nothing better to expect, as a finale to my adventure, than being dashed into atoms against the rugged surface of the satellite. And, indeed, I had now every reason to be terrified. My distance from the moon was comparatively trifling, while the labor required by the condenser was diminished not at all, and I could discover no indication whatever of a decreasing rarity in the air.

April 19th. This morning, to my great joy, about nine o'clock, the surface of the moon being frightfully near, and my apprehensions excited to the utmost, the pump of my condenser at length gave evident tokens of an alteration in the atmosphere. By ten, I had reason to believe its density considerably increased. By eleven, very little labor was necessary at the apparatus; and at twelve o'clock, with some hesitation, I ventured to unscrew the tourniquet, when, finding no inconvenience from having done so, I finally threw open the gum-elastic chamber, and unrigged it from around the car. As might have been expected, spasms and violent headache were the immediate consequences of an experiment so precipitate and full of danger. But these and other difficulties attending respiration, as they were by no means so great as to put me in peril of my life, I determined to endure as I best could, in consideration of my leaving them behind me momently in my approach to the denser strata near the moon. This approach, however, was still impetuous in the extreme; and it soon became alarmingly certain that, although I had probably not been deceived in the expectation of an atmosphere dense in proportion to the mass of the satellite, still I had been wrong in supposing this density, even at the surface, at all adequate to the support of the great weight contained in the car of my balloon. Yet this should have been the case, and in an equal degree as at the surface of the earth, the actual gravity of bodies at either planet supposed in the ratio of the atmospheric condensation. That it was not the case, however, my precipitous downfall gave testimony enough; why it was not so, can only be explained by a reference to those possible geological disturbances to which I have formerly alluded. At all events I was now close upon the planet, and coming down with the most terrible impetuosity. I lost not a moment, accordingly, in throwing overboard first my ballast, then my water-kegs, then my condensing apparatus and gum-elastic chamber, and finally every article within the car. But it was all to no purpose. I still fell with horrible rapidity, and was now not more than half a mile from the surface. As a last resource, therefore, having got rid of my coat, hat, and boots, I cut loose from the balloon the car itself, which was of no inconsiderable weight, and thus, clinging with both hands to the net-work, I had barely time to observe that the whole country, as far as the eye could reach, was thickly interspersed with diminutive habitations, ere I tumbled headlong into the very heart of a fantastical-looking city, and into the middle of a vast crowd of ugly little people, who none of them uttered a single syllable, or gave themselves the least trouble to render me assistance, but stood, like a parcel of idiots, grinning in a ludicrous manner, and eyeing me and my balloon askant, with their arms set a-kimbo. I turned from them in contempt, and, gazing upward at the earth so lately left, and left perhaps for ever, beheld it like a huge, dull, copper shield, about two degrees in diameter, fixed immovably in the heavens overhead, and tipped on one of its edges with a crescent border of the most brilliant gold. No traces of land or water could be discovered, and the whole was clouded with variable spots, and belted with tropical and equatorial zones.

Thus, may it please your Excellencies, after a series of great anxieties, unheard of dangers, and unparalleled escapes, I had, at length, on the nineteenth day of my departure from Rotterdam, arrived in safety at the conclusion of a voyage undoubtedly the most extraordinary, and the most momentous, ever accomplished, undertaken, or conceived by any denizen of earth. But my adventures yet remain to be related. And indeed your Excellencies may well imagine that, after a residence of five years upon a planet not only deeply interesting in its own peculiar character, but rendered doubly so by its intimate connection, in capacity of satellite, with the world inhabited by man, I may have intelligence for the private ear of the States' College of Astronomers of far more importance than the details, however wonderful, of the mere voyage which so happily concluded. This is, in fact, the case. I have much — very much which it would give me the greatest pleasure to communicate. I have much to say of the climate of the planet; of its wonderful alternations of heat and cold, of unmitigated and burning sunshine for one fortnight, and more than polar frigidity for the next; of a constant transfer of moisture, by distillation like that in vacuo, from the point beneath the sun to the point the farthest from it; of a variable zone of running water, of the people themselves; of their manners, customs, and political institutions; of their peculiar physical construction; of their ugliness; of their want of ears, those useless appendages in an atmosphere so peculiarly modified; of their consequent ignorance of the use and properties of speech; of their substitute for speech in a singular method of inter-communication; of the incomprehensible connection between each particular individual in the moon with some particular individual on the earth — a connection analogous with, and depending upon, that of the orbs of the planet and the satellites, and by means of which the lives and destinies of the inhabitants of the one are interwoven with the lives and destinies of the inhabitants of the other; and above all, if it so please your Excellencies — above all, of those dark and hideous mysteries which lie in the outer regions of the moon — regions which, owing to the almost miraculous accordance of the satellite's rotation on its own axis with its sidereal revolution about the earth, have never yet been turned, and, by God's mercy, never shall be turned, to the scrutiny of the telescopes of man. All this, and more — much more — would I most willingly detail. But, to be brief, I must have my reward. I am pining for a return to my family and to my home, and as the price of any farther communication on my part — in consideration of the light which I have it in my power to throw upon many very important branches of physical and metaphysical science — I must solicit, through the influence of your honorable body, a pardon for the crime of which I have been guilty in the death of the creditors upon my departure from Rotterdam. This, then, is the object of the present paper. Its bearer, an inhabitant of the moon, whom I have prevailed upon, and properly instructed, to be my messenger to the earth, will await your Excellencies' pleasure, and return to me with the pardon in question, if it can, in any manner, be obtained.

I have the honor to be, etc., your Excellencies' very humble servant,

HANS PFAALL.

Upon finishing the perusal of this very extraordinary document, Professor Rub-a-dub, it is said, dropped his pipe upon the ground in the extremity of his surprise, and Mynheer Superbus Von Underduk having taken off his spectacles, wiped them, and deposited them in his pocket, so far forgot both himself and his dignity, as to turn round three times upon his heel in the quintessence of astonishment and admiration. There was no doubt about the matter — the pardon should be obtained. So at least swore, with a round oath, Professor Rub-a-dub, and so finally thought the illustrious Von Underduk, as he took the arm of his brother in science, and without saying a word, began to make the best of his way home to deliberate upon the measures to be adopted. Having reached the door, however, of the burgomaster's dwelling, the professor ventured to suggest that as the messenger had thought proper to disappear — no doubt frightened to death by the savage appearance of the burghers of Rotterdam — the pardon would be of little use, as no one but a man of the moon would undertake a voyage to so vast a distance. To the truth of this observation the burgomaster assented, and the matter was therefore at an end. Not so, however, rumors and speculations. The letter, having been published, gave rise to a variety of gossip and opinion. Some of the over-wise even made themselves ridiculous by decrying the whole business; as nothing better than a hoax. But hoax, with these sort of people, is, I believe, a general term for all matters above their comprehension. For my part, I cannot conceive upon what data they have founded such an accusation. Let us see what they say:

Imprimus. That certain wags in Rotterdam have certain especial antipathies to certain burgomasters and astronomers.

Don't understand at all.

Secondly. That an odd little dwarf and bottle conjurer, both of whose ears, for some misdemeanor, have been cut off close to his head, has been missing for several days from the neighboring city of Bruges.

Well — what of that?

Thirdly. That the newspapers which were stuck all over the little balloon were newspapers of Holland, and therefore could not have been made in the moon. They were dirty papers — very dirty — and Gluck, the printer, would take his Bible oath to their having been printed in Rotterdam.

He was mistaken — undoubtedly — mistaken.

Fourthly. That Hans Pfaall himself, the drunken villain, and the three very idle gentlemen styled his creditors, were all seen, no longer than two or three days ago, in a tippling house in the suburbs, having just returned, with money in their pockets, from a trip beyond the sea. Don't believe it — don't believe a word of it. Lastly. That it is an opinion very generally received, or which ought to be generally received, that the College of Astronomers in the city of Rotterdam, as well as other colleges in all other parts of the world, — not to mention colleges and astronomers in general, — are, to say the least of the matter, not a whit better, nor greater, nor wiser than they ought to be.

Endnotes

1.The zodiacal light is probably what the ancients called Trabes. Emicant Trabes quos docos vocant. — Pliny, lib. 2, p. 26.

2.Since the original publication of Hans Pfaall, I find that Mr. Green, of Nassau balloon notoriety, and other late aeronauts, deny the assertions of Humboldt, in this respect, and speak of a decreasing inconvenience, — precisely in accordance with the theory here urged in a mere spirit of banter.

3.Havelius writes that he has several times found, in skies perfectly clear, when even stars of the sixth and seventh magnitude were conspicuous, that, at the same altitude of the moon, at the same elongation from the earth, and with one and the same excellent telescope, the moon and its maculae did not appear equally lucid at all times. From the circumstances of the observation, it is evident that the cause of this phenomenon is not either in our air, in the tube, in the moon, or in the eye of the spectator, but must be looked for in something (an atmosphere?) existing about the moon.

Commentary by Edgar Allan Poe on Hans Pfaall

Strictly speaking, there is but little similarity between the above sketchy trifle and the celebrated "Moon-Story" of Mr. Locke; but as both have the character of *hoaxes,* (although the one is in a tone of banter, the other of downright earnest), and as both hoaxes are on the same subject, the moon – moreover, as both attempt to give plausibility by scientific detail – the author of "Hans Pfaall" thinks it necessary to say, in *self-defence*, that his own *jeu d'esprit* was published in the "Southern Literary Messenger" about three weeks before the commencement of Mr. L's in the "New York Sun." Fancying a likeness which, perhaps, does not exist, some of the New York papers copied "Hans Pfaall," and collated it with the "Moon-Hoax," by way of detecting the writer of the one in the writer of the other.

As many more persons were actually gulled by the "Moon-Hoax" than would be willing to acknowledge the fact, it may here afford some little amusement to show why no one should have been deceived – to point out those particulars of the story which should have been sufficient to establish its real character. Indeed, however rich the imagination displayed in this ingenious fiction, it wanted much of the force which might have been given it by a more scrupulous attention to facts and to general analogy. That the public were misled, even for an instant, merely proves the gross ignorance which is so generally prevalent upon subjects of an astronomical nature.

The moon's distance from the earth is, in round numbers, 240,000 miles. If we desire to ascertain how near, apparently, a lens would bring the satellite (or any distant object), we, of course, have but to divide the distance by the magnifying or, more strictly, by the space-penetrating power of the glass. Mr. L. makes his lens have a power of 42,000 times. By this divide 240,000 (the moon's real distance), and we have five miles and five sevenths, as the apparent distance. No animal at all could be seen so far; much less the minute points particularized in the story. Mr. L. speaks about Sir John Herschel's perceiving flowers (the Papaver rheas, etc.), and even detecting the color and the shape of the eyes of small birds. Shortly before, too, he has himself observed that the lens would not render perceptible objects of less than eighteen inches in diameter; but even this, as I have said, is giving the glass by far too great power. It may be observed, in passing, that this prodigious glass is said to have been moulded at the glasshouse of Messrs. Hartley and Grant, in Dumbarton; but Messrs. H. and G.'s establishment had ceased operations for many years previous to the publication of the hoax.

On page 13, pamphlet edition, speaking of "a hairy veil" over the eyes of a species of bison, the author says: "It immediately occurred to the acute mind of Dr. Herschel that this was a providential contrivance to protect the eyes of the animal from the great extremes of light and darkness to which all the inhabitants of our side of the moon are periodically subjected." But this cannot be thought a very "acute" observation of the Doctor's. The inhabitants of our side of the moon have, evidently, no darkness at all, so there can be nothing of the "extremes" mentioned. In the absence of the sun they have a light from the earth equal to that of thirteen full unclouded moons.

The topography throughout, even when professing to accord with Blunt's Lunar Chart, is entirely at variance with that or any other lunar chart, and even grossly at variance with itself. The points of the compass, too, are in inextricable confusion; the writer appearing to be ignorant that, on a lunar map, these are not in accordance with terrestrial points; the east being to the left, etc.

Deceived, perhaps, by the vague titles, Mare Nubium, Mare Tranquillitatis, Mare Faecunditatis, etc., given to the dark spots by former astronomers, Mr. L. has entered into details regarding oceans and other large bodies of water in the moon; whereas there is no astronomical point more positively ascertained than that no such bodies exist there. In examining the boundary between light and darkness (in the crescent or gibbous moon) where this boundary crosses any of the dark places, the line of division is found to be rough and jagged; but, were these dark places liquid, it would evidently be even.

The description of the wings of the man-bat, on page 21, is but a literal copy of Peter Wilkins' account of the wings of his flying islanders. This simple fact should have induced suspicion, at least, it might be thought.

On page 23, we have the following: "What a prodigious influence must our thirteen times larger globe have exercised upon this satellite when an embryo in the womb of time, the passive subject of chemical affinity!" This is very fine; but it should be observed that no astronomer would have made such remark, especially to any journal of Science; for the earth, in the sense intended, is not only thirteen, but forty-nine times larger than the moon. A similar objection applies to the whole of the concluding pages, where, by way of introduction to some discoveries in Saturn, the philosophical correspondent enters into a minute schoolboy account of that planet – this to the "Edinburgh journal of Science!"

But there is one point, in particular, which should have betrayed the fiction. Let us imagine the power actually possessed of seeing animals upon the moon's surface; – what would first arrest the attention of an observer from the earth? Certainly neither their shape, size, nor any other such peculiarity, so soon as their remarkable *situation*. They would appear to be walking, with heels up and head down, in the manner of flies on a ceiling. The *real* observer would have uttered an instant ejaculation of surprise (however prepared by previous knowledge) at the singularity of their position; the *fictitious* observer has not even mentioned the subject, but speaks of seeing the entire bodies of such creatures, when it is demonstrable that he could have seen only the diameter of their heads!

It might as well be remarked, in conclusion, that the size, and particularly the powers of the man-bats (for example, their ability to fly in so rare an atmosphere – if, indeed, the moon have any) with most of the other fancies in regard to animal and vegetable existence, are at variance, generally, with all analogical reasoning on these themes; and that analogy here will often amount to conclusive demonstration. It is, perhaps, scarcely necessary to add, that all the suggestions attributed to Brewster and Herschel, in the beginning of the article, about "a transfusion of artificial light through the focal object of vision," etc., etc., belong to that species of figurative writing which comes, most properly, under the denomination of rigmarole.

There is a real and very definite limit to optical discovery among the stars – a limit whose nature need only be stated to be understood. If, indeed, the casting of large lenses were all that is required, man's ingenuity would ultimately prove equal to the task, and we might have them of any size demanded. But, unhappily, in proportion to the increase of size in the lens, and consequently of space-penetrating power, is the diminution of light from the object, by diffusion of its rays. And for this evil there is no remedy within human ability; for an object is seen by means of that light alone which proceeds from itself, whether direct or reflected. Thus the only "*artificial*" light which could avail Mr. Locke, would be some artificial light which he should be able to throw – not upon the "focal object of vision," but upon the real object to be viewed – to wit: *upon the moon*. It has been easily calculated that, when the light proceeding from a star becomes so diffused as to be as weak as the natural light proceeding from the whole of the stars, in a clear and moonless night, then the star is no longer visible for any practical purpose.

The Earl of Ross's telescope, lately constructed in England, has a *speculum* with a reflecting surface of 4,071 square inches; the Herschel telescope having one of only

1,811. The metal of the Earl of Ross's is 6 feet diameter; it is 5 1/2 inches thick at the edges, and 5 at the centre. The weight is 3 tons. The focal length is 50 feet.

I have lately read a singular and somewhat ingenious little book, whose title-page runs thus: "L'Homme dans la lvne ou le Voyage Chimerique fait au Monde de la Lvne, nouuellement decouuert par Dominique Gonzales, Aduanturier Espagnol, autremét dit le Courier volant. Mis en notre langve par J. B. D. A. Paris, chez Francois Piot, pres la Fontaine de Saint Benoist. Et chez J. Goignard, au premier pilier de la grand' salle du Palais, proche les Consultations, MDCXLVIII." pp. 76.

The writer professes to have translated his work from the English of one Mr. D'Avisson (Davidson?) although there is a terrible ambiguity in the statement. "J'en ai eu," says he "l'original de Monsieur D'Avisson, medecin des mieux versez qui soient aujourd'huy dans la cònoissance des Belles Lettres, et sur tout de la Philosophic Naturelle. Je lui ai cette obligation entre les autres, de m' auoir non seulement mis en main cc Livre en anglois, mais encore le Manuscrit du Sieur Thomas D'Anan, gentilhomme Eccossois, recommandable pour sa vertu, sur la version duquel j' advoue que j' ay tiré le plan de la mienne."

After some irrelevant adventures, much in the manner of Gil Blas, and which occupy the first thirty pages, the author relates that, being ill during a sea voyage, the crew abandoned him, together with a negro servant, on the island of St. Helena. To increase the chances of obtaining food, the two separate, and live as far apart as possible. This brings about a training of birds, to serve the purpose of carrier-pigeons between them. By and by these are taught to carry parcels of some weight – and this weight is gradually increased. At length the idea is entertained of uniting the force of a great number of the birds, with a view to raising the author himself. A machine is contrived for the purpose, and we have a minute description of it, which is materially helped out by a steel engraving. Here we perceive the Signor Gonzales, with point ruffles and a huge periwig, seated astride something which resembles very closely a broomstick, and borne aloft by a multitude of wild swans (*ganzas*) who had strings reaching from their tails to the machine.

The main event detailed in the Signor's narrative depends upon a very important fact, of which the reader is kept in ignorance until near the end of the book. The *ganzas*, with whom he had become so familiar, were not really denizens of St. Helena, but of the moon. Thence it had been their custom, time out of mind, to migrate annually to some portion of the earth. In proper season, of course, they would return home; and the author, happening, one day, to require their services for a short voyage, is unexpectedly carried straight up, and in a very brief period arrives at the satellite. Here he finds, among other odd things, that the people enjoy extreme happiness; that they have no *law*; that they die without pain; that they are from ten to thirty feet in height; that they live five thousand years; that they have an emperor called Irdonozur; and that they can jump sixty feet high, when, being out of the gravitating influence, they fly about with fans.

I cannot forbear giving a specimen of the general

philosophy of the volume.

"I must now declare to you," says the Signor Gonzales, "the nature of the place in which I found myself. All the clouds were beneath my feet, or, if you please, spread between me and the earth. As to the stars, *since there was no night where I was, they always had the same appearance; not brilliant, as usual, but pale, and very nearly like the moon of a morning.* But few of them were visible, and these ten times larger (as well as I could judge), than they seem to the inhabitants of the earth. The moon, which wanted two days of being full, was of a terrible bigness.

"I must not forget here, that the stars appeared only on that side of the globe turned towards the moon, and that the closer they were to it the larger they seemed. I have also to inform you that, whether it was calm weather or stormy, I found myself *always immediately between the moon and the earth.* I was convinced of this for two reasons because my birds always flew in a straight line; and because whenever we attempted to rest, we were carried insensibly around the globe of the earth. For I admit the opinion of Copernicus, who maintains that it never ceases to revolve *from the east to the west*, not upon the poles of the Equinoctial, commonly called the poles of the world, but upon those of the Zodiac, a question of which I propose to speak more at length hereafter, when I shall have leisure to refresh my memory in regard to the astrology which I learned at Salamanca when young, and have since forgotten."

Notwithstanding the blunders italicized, the book is not

without some claim to attention, as affording a naive specimen of the current astronomical notions of the time. One of these assumed, that the "gravitating power" extended but a short distance from the earth's surface, and, accordingly, we find our voyager "carried insensibly around the globe," etc.

There have been other "voyages to the moon," but none of higher merit than the one just mentioned. That of Bergerac is utterly meaningless. In the third volume of the "American Quarterly Review" will be found quite an elaborate criticism upon a certain "Journey" of the kind in question; a criticism in which it is difficult to say whether the critic most exposes the stupidity of the book, or his own absurd ignorance of astronomy. I forget the title of the work; but the *means* of the voyage are more deplorably ill conceived than are even the *ganzas* of our friend the Signor Gonzales. The adventurer, in digging the earth, happens to discover a peculiar metal for which the moon has a strong attraction, and straightway constructs of it a box, which, when cast loose from its terrestrial fastenings, flies with him forthwith to the satellite. The "Flight of Thomas O'Rourke" is a jeu d'esprit not altogether contemptible, and has been translated into German. Thomas, the hero, was, in fact, the gamekeeper of an Irish peer, whose eccentricities gave rise to the tale. The "flight" is made on an eagle's back, from Hungry Hill, a lofty mountain at the end of Bantry Bay.

In these various brochures the aim is always satirical, the theme being a description of Lunarian customs as compared with ours. In none is there any effort of *plausibility* in the details of the voyage itself. The writers seem in each instance to be utterly uninformed in respect to astronomy. In "Hans Pfaall" the design is original, inasmuch as regards an attempt at *verisimilitude*, in the application of scientific principles (so far as the whimsical nature of the subject would permit), to the actual passage between the earth and the moon.

The Conversation of Eiros and Charmion

Edgar Allan Poe

Introduction

Edgar Allan Poe's apocalyptic tale *The Conversation of Eiros and Charmion* was first published in Burton's Gentleman's Magazine in 1839. In this story, two human spirits discuss the recent end of the world. Eiros, who died in this apocalypse, tells Charmion, who had died ten years previously, how the end came about, and how the human race was wiped out.

The Conversation of Eiros and Charmion

Edgar Allan Poe

I will bring fire to thee.
– Euripides, Andromache

EIROS: Why do you call me Eiros?

CHARMION: So henceforth will you always be called. You must forget too, my earthly name, and speak to me as Charmion.

EIROS: This is indeed no dream!

CHARMION: Dreams are with us no more;– but of these mysteries anon. I rejoice to see you looking life-like and rational. The film of the shadow has already passed from off your eyes. Be of heart and fear nothing. Your allotted days of stupor have expired and, to-morrow, I will myself induct you into the full joys and wonders of your novel existence.

EIROS: True – I feel no stupor – none at all. The wild sickness and the terrible darkness have left me, and I hear no longer that mad, rushing, horrible sound, like the "voice of many waters". Yet my senses are bewildered, Charmion, with the keenness of their perception of the new.

CHARMION: A few days will remove all this;– but I fully understand you, and feel for you. It is now ten earthly years since I underwent what you undergo – yet the remembrance of it hangs by me still. You have now suffered all of pain, however, which you will suffer in Aidenn.

EIROS: In Aidenn?

CHARMION: In Aidenn.

EIROS: Oh, God!– pity me, Charmion!– I am overburthened with the majesty of all things – of the unknown now known – of the speculative Future merged in the august and certain Present.

CHARMION: Grapple not now with such thoughts. To-morrow we will speak of this. Your mind wavers, and its agitation will find relief in the exercise of simple memories. Look not around, nor forward – but back. I am burning with anxiety to hear the details of that stupendous event which threw you among us. Tell me of it. Let us converse of familiar things, in the old familiar language of the world which has so fearfully perished.

EIROS: Most fearfully, fearfully!– this is indeed no dream.

CHARMION: Dreams are no more. Was I much mourned,

my Eiros?

EIROS: Mourned, Charmion?– oh deeply. To that last hour of all, there hung a cloud of intense gloom and devout sorrow over your household.

CHARMION: And that last hour – speak of it. Remember that, beyond the naked fact of the catastrophe itself, I know nothing. When, coming out from among mankind, I passed into Night through the Grave – at that period, if I remember aright, the calamity which overwhelmed you was utterly unanticipated. But, indeed, I knew little of the speculative philosophy of the day.

EIROS: The individual calamity was, as you say, entirely unanticipated; but analogous misfortunes had been long a subject of discussion with astronomers. I need scarce tell you, my friend, that, even when you left us, men had agreed to understand those passages in the most holy writings which speak of the final destruction of all things by fire, as having reference to the orb of the earth alone. But in regard to the immediate agency of the ruin, speculation had been at fault from that epoch in astronomical knowledge in which the comets were divested of the terrors of flame. The very moderate density of these bodies had been well established. They had been observed to pass among the satellites of Jupiter, without bringing about any sensible alteration either in the masses or in the orbits of these secondary planets. We had long regarded the wanderers as vapory creations of inconceivable tenuity, and as altogether incapable of doing injury to our substantial globe, even in the event of contact. But contact was not in any degree dreaded; for the elements of all the comets were accurately known. That among them we should look for the agency of the threatened fiery destruction had been for many years considered an inadmissible idea. But wonders and wild fancies had been, of late days, strangely rife among mankind; and, although it was only with a few of the ignorant that actual apprehension prevailed, upon the announcement by astronomers of a new comet, yet this announcement was generally received with I know not what of agitation and mistrust.

The elements of the strange orb were immediately calculated, and it was at once conceded by all observers, that its path, at perihelion, would bring it into very close proximity with the earth. There were two or three astronomers, of secondary note, who resolutely maintained that a contact was inevitable. I cannot very well express to you the effect of this intelligence upon the people. For a few short days they would not believe an assertion which their intellect, so long employed among worldly considerations, could not in any manner grasp. But the truth of a vitally important fact soon makes its way into the understanding of even the most stolid. Finally, all men saw that astronomical knowledge lied not, and they awaited the comet. Its approach was not, at first, seemingly rapid; nor was its appearance of very unusual character. It was of a dull red, and had little perceptible train. For seven or eight days we saw no material increase in its apparent diameter, and but a partial alteration in its color. Meantime the ordinary affairs of men were discarded, and all interests absorbed in a growing discussion, instituted by the philosophic, in respect to the cometary nature. Even the grossly ignorant aroused their sluggish capacities to such considerations. The learned now gave their intellect – their soul – to no such points as the allaying of fear, or to the sustenance of loved theory. They sought – they panted for right views. They groaned for perfected knowledge. Truth arose in the purity of her strength and exceeding majesty, and the wise bowed down and adored.

That material injury to our globe or to its inhabitants would result from the apprehended contact, was an opinion which hourly lost ground among the wise; and the wise were now freely permitted to rule the reason and the fancy of the crowd. It was demonstrated, that the density of the comet's nucleus was far less than that of our rarest gas; and the harmless passage of a similar visitor among the satellites of Jupiter was a point strongly insisted upon, and which served greatly to allay terror. Theologists, with an earnestness fear-enkindled, dwelt upon the biblical prophecies, and expounded them to the people with a directness and simplicity of which no previous instance had been known. That the final destruction of the earth must be brought about by the agency of fire, was urged with a spirit that enforced everywhere conviction; and that the comets were of no fiery nature (as all men now knew) was a truth which relieved all, in a great measure, from the apprehension of the great calamity foretold. It is noticeable that the popular prejudices and vulgar errors in regard to pestilences and wars – errors which were wont to prevail upon every appearance of a comet – were now altogether unknown. As if by some sudden convulsive exertion, reason had at once hurled superstition from her throne. The feeblest intellect had derived vigor from excessive interest.

What minor evils might arise from the contact were points of elaborate question. The learned spoke of slight geological disturbances, of probable alterations in climate, and consequently in vegetation, of possible magnetic and electric influences. Many held that no visible or perceptible effect would in any manner be produced. While such discussions were going on, their subject gradually approached, growing larger in apparent diameter, and of a more brilliant lustre. Mankind grew paler as it came. All human operations were suspended. There was an epoch in the course of the general sentiment when the comet had attained, at length, a size surpassing that of any previously recorded visitation. The people now, dismissing any lingering hope that the astronomers were wrong, experienced all the certainty of evil. The chimerical aspect of their terror was gone. The hearts of the stoutest of our race beat violently within their bosoms. A very few days sufficed, however, to merge even such feelings in sentiments more unendurable. We could no longer apply to the strange orb any accustomed thoughts. Its historical attributes had disappeared. It oppressed us with a hideous novelty of emotion. We saw it not as an astronomical phenomenon in the heavens, but as an incubus upon our hearts, and a shadow upon our brains. It had taken, with inconceivable rapidity, the character of a gigantic mantle of rare flame, extending from horizon to horizon.

Yet a day, and men breathed with greater freedom. It was clear that we were already within the influence of the comet; yet we lived. We even felt an unusual elasticity of frame and vivacity of mind. The exceeding tenuity of the object of our dread was apparent; for all heavenly objects were plainly visible through it. Meantime, our vegetation had perceptibly altered; and we gained faith, from this predicted circumstance, in the foresight of the wise. A wild luxuriance of foliage, utterly unknown before, burst out upon every vegetable thing.

Yet another day, and the evil was not altogether upon us. It was now evident that its nucleus would first reach us. A wild change had come over all men; and the first sense of pain was the wild signal for general lamentation and horror. This first sense of pain lay in a rigorous constriction of the breast and lungs, and an insufferable dryness of the skin. It could not be denied that our atmosphere was radically affected; the conformation of this atmosphere and the possible modifications to which it might be subjected, were now the topics of discussion. The result of investigation sent an electric thrill of the intensest terror through the universal heart of man.

It had been long known that the air which encircled us was a compound of oxygen and nitrogen gases, in the proportion of twenty-one measures of oxygen, and seventy-nine of nitrogen, in every one hundred of the atmosphere. Oxygen, which was the principle of combustion, and the vehicle of heat, was absolutely necessary to the support of animal life, and was the most powerful and energetic agent in nature. Nitrogen, on the contrary, was incapable of supporting either animal life or flame. An unnatural excess of oxygen would result, it had been ascertained, in just such an elevation of the animal spirits as we had latterly experienced. It was the pursuit, the extension of the idea, which had engendered awe. What would be the result of a total extraction of the nitrogen? A combustion irresistible, all-devouring, omni-prevalent, immediate;– the entire fulfillment, in all their minute and terrible details, of the fiery and horror-inspiring denunciations of the prophecies of the Holy Book.

Why need I paint, Charmion, the now disenchained frenzy of mankind? That tenuity in the comet which had previously inspired us with hope, was now the source of the bitterness of despair. In its impalpable gaseous character we clearly perceived the consummation of Fate. Meantime a day again passed, bearing away with it the last shadow of Hope. We gasped in the rapid modification of the air. The red blood bounded tumultuously through its strict channels. A furious delirium possessed all men; and, with arms rigidly outstretched toward the threatening heavens, they trembled and shrieked aloud. But the nucleus of the destroyer was now upon us; even here in Aidenn, I shudder while I speak. Let me be brief– brief as the ruin that overwhelmed. For a moment there was a wild lurid light alone, visiting and penetrating all things. Then – let us bow down, Charmion, before the excessive majesty of the great God!– then, there came a shouting and pervading sound, as if from the mouth itself of HIM; while the whole incumbent mass of ether in which we existed, burst at once into a species of intense flame, for whose surpassing brilliancy and all-fervid heat even the angels in the high Heaven of pure knowledge have no name. Thus ended all.

The Birthmark

Nathaniel Hawthorne

Introduction

Nathaniel Hawthorne (1804–1864) was born in Salem, Massachusetts, and is perhaps most famous for his novel *The Scarlet Letter*. *The Birthmark* tells of a scientist who becomes so repulsed by the small blemish on his wife's cheek that he seeks to create the cure, but his desire to rid his wife of this minor disfigurement leads to devastating consequences.

First published in March 1843, this could be said to be one of the earliest works in the "mad scientist" sub-genre.

The Birthmark

Nathaniel Hawthorne

In the latter part of the last century there lived a man of science, an eminent proficient in every branch of natural philosophy, who not long before our story opens had made experience of a spiritual affinity more attractive than any chemical one. He had left his laboratory to the care of an assistant, cleared his fine countenance from the furnace-smoke, washed the stain of acids from his fingers, and persuaded a beautiful woman to become his wife. In those days when the comparatively recent discovery of electricity and other kindred mysteries of Nature seemed to open paths into the region of miracle, it was not unusual for the love of science to rival the love of woman in its depth and absorbing energy. The higher intellect, the imagination, the spirit, and even the heart might all find their congenial aliment in pursuits which, as some of their ardent votaries believed, would ascend from one step of powerful intelligence to another, until the philosopher should lay his hand on the secret of creative force and perhaps make new worlds for himself. We know not whether Aylmer possessed this degree of faith in man's ultimate control over Nature. He had devoted himself, however, too unreservedly to scientific studies ever to be weaned from them by any second passion. His love for his young wife might prove the stronger of the two; but it could only be by intertwining itself with his love of science and uniting the strength of the latter to his own.

Such a union accordingly took place, and was attended with truly remarkable consequences and a deeply impressive moral. One day, very soon after their marriage, Aylmer sat gazing at his wife with a trouble in his countenance that grew stronger until he spoke.

"Georgiana," said he, "has it never occurred to you that the mark upon your cheek might be removed?"

"No, indeed," said she, smiling; but perceiving the seriousness of his manner, she blushed deeply. "To tell you the truth it has been so often called a charm, that I was simple enough to imagine it might be so."

"Ah, upon another face perhaps it might," replied her husband; "but never on yours. No, dearest Georgiana, you came so nearly perfect from the hand of Nature, that this slightest possible defect, which we hesitate whether to term a defect or a beauty, shocks me, as being the visible mark of earthly imperfection."

"Shocks you, my husband!" cried Georgiana, deeply hurt; at first reddening with momentary anger, but then bursting into tears. "Then why did you take me from my mother's side? You cannot love what shocks you!"

To explain this conversation, it must be mentioned that in the centre of Georgiana's left cheek there was a singular mark, deeply interwoven, as it were, with the texture and substance of her face. In the usual state of her complexion – a healthy though delicate bloom – the mark wore a tint of deeper crimson, which imperfectly defined its shape amid the surrounding rosiness. When she blushed it gradually became more indistinct, and finally vanished amid the triumphant rush of blood that bathed the whole cheek with its brilliant glow. But if any shifting motion caused her to turn pale there was the mark again, a crimson stain upon the snow, in what Aylmer sometimes deemed an almost fearful distinctness. Its shape bore not a little similarity to the human hand, though of the smallest pygmy size. Georgiana's lovers were wont to say that some fairy at her birth hour had laid her tiny hand upon the infant's cheek, and left this impress there in token of the magic endowments that were to give her such sway over all hearts. Many a desperate swain would have risked life for the privilege of pressing his lips to the mysterious hand. It must not be concealed, however, that the impression wrought by this fairy sign-manual varied exceedingly, according to the difference of temperament in the beholders. Some fastidious persons – but they were exclusively of her own sex – affirmed that the bloody hand, as they chose to call it, quite destroyed the effect of Georgiana's beauty and rendered her countenance even hideous. But it would be as reasonable to say that one of those small blue stains which sometimes occur in the purest statuary marble would convert the Eve of Powers to a monster. Masculine observers, if the birthmark did not heighten their admiration, contented themselves with wishing it away, that the world might possess one living specimen of ideal loveliness without the semblance of a flaw. After his marriage, for he thought little or nothing of the matter before, Aylmer discovered that this was the case with himself.

Had she been less beautiful, if Envy's self could have found aught else to sneer at, he might have felt his affection heightened by the prettiness of this mimic hand, now vaguely portrayed, now lost, now stealing forth again and glimmering to and fro with every pulse of emotion that throbbed within her heart; but, seeing her otherwise so perfect, he found this one defect grow more and more intolerable with every moment of their united lives. It was the fatal flaw of humanity which Nature, in one shape or another, stamps ineffaceably on all her productions, either to imply that they are temporary and finite, or that their perfection must be wrought by toil and pain. The crimson hand expressed the ineludible gripe in which mortality clutches the highest and purest of earthly mould, degrading them into kindred with the lowest, and even with the very brutes, like whom their visible frames return to dust. In this manner, selecting it as the symbol of his wife's liability to sin, sorrow, decay, and death, Aylmer's sombre imagination was not long in rendering the birthmark a frightful object, causing him more trouble and horror than ever Georgiana's beauty, whether of soul or sense, had given him delight.

At all the seasons which should have been their happiest he invariably, and without intending it, nay, in spite of a purpose to the contrary, reverted to this one disastrous topic. Trifling as it at first appeared, it so connected itself with innumerable trains of thought and modes of feeling that it became the central point of all. With the morning twilight Aylmer opened his eyes upon his wife's face and recognized the symbol of imperfection; and when they sat together at the evening hearth his eyes wandered stealthily to her cheek, and beheld, flickering with the blaze of the wood fire, the spectral hand that wrote mortality where he would fain have worshipped. Georgiana soon learned to shudder at his gaze. It needed but a glance with the peculiar expression that his face often wore to change the roses of her cheek into a death-like paleness, amid which the crimson hand was brought strongly out, like a bas-relief of ruby on the whitest marble.

Late one night when the lights were growing dim so as hardly to betray the stain on the poor wife's cheek, she herself, for the first time, voluntarily took up the subject.

"Do you remember, my dear Aylmer," said she, with a feeble attempt at a smile, "have you any recollection, of a dream last night about this odious hand?"

"None! none whatever!" replied Aylmer, starting; but then he added, in a dry, cold tone, affected for the sake of concealing the real depth of his emotion, "I might well dream of it; for before I fell asleep, it had taken a pretty firm hold of my fancy."

"And you did dream of it?" continued Georgiana, hastily; for she dreaded lest a gush of tears should interrupt what she had to say. "A terrible dream! I wonder that you can forget it. Is it possible to forget this one expression? – 'It is in her heart now; we must have it out!' Reflect, my husband; for by all means I would have you recall that dream."

The mind is in a sad state when Sleep, the all-involving, cannot confine her spectres within the dim region of her sway, but suffers them to break forth, affrighting this actual life with secrets that perchance belong to a deeper one. Aylmer now remembered his dream. He had fancied himself with his servant Aminadab, attempting an operation for the removal of the birthmark; but the deeper went the knife, the deeper sank the hand, until at length its tiny grasp appeared to have caught hold of Georgiana's heart; whence, however, her husband was inexorably resolved to cut or wrench it away.

When the dream had shaped itself perfectly in his memory, Aylmer sat in his wife's presence with a guilty feeling. Truth often finds its way to the mind close muffled in robes of sleep, and then speaks with uncompromising directness of matters in regard to which we practise an unconscious self-deception during our waking moments. Until now, he had not been aware of the tyrannizing influence acquired by one idea over his mind, and of the lengths which he might find in his heart to go for the sake of giving himself peace.

"Aylmer," resumed Georgiana, solemnly, "I know not what may be the cost to both of us to rid me of this fatal birthmark. Perhaps its removal may cause cureless deformity; or it may be the stain goes as deep as life itself. Again: do we know that there is a possibility, on any terms, of unclasping the firm gripe of this little hand which was laid upon me before I came into the world?"

"Dearest Georgiana, I have spent much thought upon the subject," hastily interrupted Aylmer. "I am convinced of the perfect practicability of its removal."

"If there be the remotest possibility of it," continued Georgiana, "let the attempt be made at whatever risk.

Danger is nothing to me; for life, while this hateful mark makes me the object of your horror and disgust, life is a burden which I would fling down with joy. Either remove this dreadful hand, or take my wretched life! You have deep science. All the world bears witness of it. You have achieved great wonders. Cannot you remove this little, little mark, which I cover with the tips of two small fingers? Is this beyond your power, for the sake of your own peace, and to save your poor wife from madness?"

"Noblest, dearest, tenderest wife," cried Aylmer, rapturously, "doubt not my power. I have already given this matter the deepest thought – thought which might almost have enlightened me to create a being less perfect than yourself. Georgiana, you have led me deeper than ever into the heart of science. I feel myself fully competent to render this dear cheek as faultless as its fellow; and then, most beloved, what will be my triumph when I shall have corrected what Nature left imperfect in her fairest work! Even Pygmalion, when his sculptured woman assumed life, felt not greater ecstasy than mine will be."

"It is resolved, then," said Georgiana, faintly smiling. "And, Aylmer, spare me not, though you should find the birthmark take refuge in my heart at last."

Her husband tenderly kissed her cheek – her right cheek – not that which bore the impress of the crimson hand.

The next day Aylmer apprised his wife of a plan that he had formed whereby he might have opportunity for the intense thought and constant watchfulness which the proposed operation would require; while Georgiana, likewise, would enjoy the perfect repose essential to its success. They were to seclude themselves in the extensive apartments occupied by Aylmer as a laboratory, and where, during his toilsome youth, he had made discoveries in the elemental powers of nature that had roused the admiration of all the learned societies in Europe. Seated calmly in this laboratory, the pale philosopher had investigated the secrets of the highest cloud-region and of the profoundest mines; he had satisfied himself of the causes that kindled and kept alive the fires of the volcano; and had explained the mystery of fountains, and how it is that they gush forth, some so bright and pure, and others with such rich medicinal virtues, from the dark bosom of the earth. Here, too, at an earlier period, he had studied the wonders of the human frame, and attempted to fathom the very process by which Nature assimilates all her precious influences from earth and air, and from the spiritual world, to create and foster man, her masterpiece. The latter pursuit, however, Aylmer had long laid aside in unwilling recognition of the truth – against which all seekers sooner or later stumble – that our great creative Mother, while she amuses us with apparently working in the broadest sunshine, is yet severely careful to keep her own secrets, and, in spite of her pretended openness, shows us nothing but results. She permits us, indeed, to mar, but seldom to mend, and, like a jealous patentee, on no account to make. Now, however, Aylmer resumed these half-forgotten investigations; not, of course, with such hopes or wishes as first suggested them; but because they involved much physiological truth and lay in the path of his proposed scheme for the treatment of Georgiana.

As he led her over the threshold of the laboratory, Georgiana was cold and tremulous. Aylmer looked cheerfully into her face, with intent to reassure her, but was so startled with the intense glow of the birthmark upon the whiteness of her cheek that he could not restrain a strong convulsive shudder. His wife fainted.

"Aminadab! Aminadab!" shouted Aylmer, stamping violently on the floor.

Forthwith there issued from an inner apartment a man of low stature, but bulky frame, with shaggy hair hanging about his visage, which was grimed with the vapors of the furnace. This personage had been Aylmer's underworker during his whole scientific career, and was admirably fitted for that office by his great mechanical readiness, and the skill with which, while incapable of comprehending a single principle, he executed all the details of his master's experiments. With his vast strength, his shaggy hair, his smoky aspect, and the indescribable earthiness that incrusted him, he seemed to represent man's physical nature; while Aylmer's slender figure, and pale, intellectual face, were no less apt a type of the spiritual element.

"Throw open the door of the boudoir, Aminadab," said Aylmer, "and burn a pastil."

"Yes, master," answered Aminadab, looking intently at the lifeless form of Georgiana; and then he muttered to himself, "If she were my wife, I'd never part with that birthmark."

When Georgiana recovered consciousness, she found herself breathing an atmosphere of penetrating fragrance, the gentle potency of which had recalled her from her death-like faintness. The scene around her looked like enchantment. Aylmer had converted those smoky, dingy, sombre rooms, where he had spent his brightest years in recondite pursuits, into a series of beautiful apartments not unfit to be the secluded abode of a lovely woman. The walls were hung with gorgeous curtains, which imparted the combination of grandeur and grace that no other species of adornment can achieve; and as they fell from the ceiling to the floor, their rich and ponderous folds, concealing all angles and straight lines, appeared to shut in the scene from infinite space. For aught Georgiana knew, it might be a pavilion among the clouds. And Aylmer, excluding the sunshine, which would have interfered with his chemical processes, had supplied its place with perfumed lamps, emitting flames of various hue, but all uniting in a soft, impurpled radiance. He now knelt by his wife's side, watching her earnestly, but without alarm; for he was confident in his science, and felt that he could draw a magic circle round her within which no evil might intrude.

"Where am I? Ah, I remember," said Georgiana, faintly; and she placed her hand over her cheek to hide the terrible mark from her husband's eyes.

"Fear not, dearest!" exclaimed he. "Do not shrink from me! Believe me, Georgiana, I even rejoice in this single imperfection, since it will be such a rapture to remove it."

"O, spare me!" sadly replied his wife. "Pray do not look at it again. I never can forget that convulsive shudder."

In order to soothe Georgiana, and, as it were, to release her mind from the burden of actual things, Aylmer now put in practice some of the light and playful secrets which science had taught him among its profounder lore. Airy figures, absolutely bodiless ideas, and forms of unsubstantial beauty came and danced before her, imprinting their momentary footsteps on beams of light. Though she had some indistinct idea of the method of these optical phenomena, still the illusion was almost perfect enough to warrant the belief that her husband possessed sway over the spiritual world. Then again, when she felt a wish to look forth from her seclusion, immediately, as if her thoughts were answered, the procession of external existence flitted across a screen. The scenery and the figures of actual life were perfectly represented, but with that bewitching yet indescribable difference which always makes a picture, an image, or a shadow so much more attractive than the original. When wearied of this, Aylmer bade her cast her eyes upon a vessel containing a quantity of earth. She did so, with little interest at first; but was soon startled to perceive the germ of a plant shooting upward from the soil. Then came the slender stalk; the leaves gradually unfolded themselves; and amid them was a perfect and lovely flower.

"It is magical!" cried Georgiana. "I dare not touch it."

"Nay, pluck it," answered Aylmer, "pluck it, and inhale its brief perfume while you may. The flower will wither in a few moments and leave nothing save its brown seed vessels; but thence may be perpetuated a race as ephemeral as itself."

But Georgiana had no sooner touched the flower than the whole plant suffered a blight, its leaves turning coal-black as if by the agency of fire.

"There was too powerful a stimulus," said Aylmer, thoughtfully.

To make up for this abortive experiment, he proposed to take her portrait by a scientific process of his own invention. It was to be effected by rays of light striking upon a polished plate of metal. Georgiana assented; but, on looking at the result, was affrighted to find the features of the portrait blurred and indefinable; while the minute figure of a hand appeared where the cheek should have been. Aylmer snatched the metallic plate and threw it into a jar of corrosive acid.

Soon, however, he forgot these mortifying failures. In the intervals of study and chemical experiment, he came to her flushed and exhausted, but seemed invigorated by her presence, and spoke in glowing language of the resources of his art. He gave a history of the long dynasty of the alchemists, who spent so many ages in quest of the universal solvent by which the golden principle might be elicited from all things vile and base. Aylmer appeared to believe that, by the plainest scientific logic, it was altogether within the limits of possibility to discover this long-sought medium.

"But," he added, "a philosopher who should go deep enough to acquire the power would attain too lofty a wisdom to stoop to the exercise of it."

Not less singular were his opinions in regard to the elixir vitæ. He more than intimated that it was at his option to concoct a liquid that should prolong life for years, perhaps interminably; but that it would produce a discord in Nature which all the world, and chiefly the quaffer of the immortal nostrum, would find cause to curse.

"Aylmer, are you in earnest?" asked Georgiana, looking at him with amazement and fear. "It is terrible to possess such power, or even to dream of possessing it."

"O, do not tremble, my love," said her husband. "I would not wrong either you or myself by working such inharmonious effects upon our lives; but I would have you consider how trifling, in comparison, is the skill requisite to remove this little hand."

At the mention of the birthmark, Georgiana, as usual, shrank as if a red-hot iron had touched her cheek.

Again Aylmer applied himself to his labors. She could hear his voice in the distant furnace room giving directions to Aminadab, whose harsh, uncouth, misshapen tones were audible in response, more like the grunt or growl of a brute than human speech. After hours of absence, Aylmer reappeared and proposed that she should now examine his cabinet of chemical products and natural treasures of the earth. Among the former he showed her a small vial, in which, he remarked, was contained a gentle yet most powerful fragrance, capable of impregnating all the breezes that blow across a kingdom. They were of inestimable value, the contents of that little vial; and, as he said so, he threw some of the perfume into the air and filled the room with piercing and invigorating delight.

"And what is this?" asked Georgiana, pointing to a small crystal globe containing a gold-colored liquid. "It is so beautiful to the eye that I could imagine it the elixir of life."

"In one sense it is," replied Aylmer; "or rather, the elixir of immortality. It is the most precious poison that ever was concocted in this world. By its aid I could apportion the lifetime of any mortal at whom you might point your finger. The strength of the dose would determine whether he were to linger out years, or drop dead in the midst of a breath. No king on his guarded throne could keep his life if I, in my private station, should deem that the welfare of millions justified me in depriving him of it."

"Why do you keep such a terrific drug?" inquired Georgiana, in horror.

"Do not mistrust me, dearest," said her husband, smiling; "its virtuous potency is yet greater than its harmful one. But see! here is a powerful cosmetic. With a few drops of this in a vase of water, freckles may be washed away as easily as the hands are cleansed. A stronger infusion would take the blood out of the cheek, and leave the rosiest beauty a pale ghost."

"Is it with this lotion that you intend to bathe my cheek?" asked Georgiana, anxiously.

"O, no," hastily replied her husband; "this is merely superficial. Your case demands a remedy that shall go deeper."

In his interviews with Georgiana, Aylmer generally made minute inquiries as to her sensations and whether the confinement of the rooms and the temperature of the atmosphere agreed with her. These questions had such a particular drift that Georgiana began to conjecture that she was already subjected to certain physical influences, either breathed in with the fragrant air or taken with her food. She fancied likewise, but it might be altogether fancy, that there was a stirring up of her system – a strange, indefinite sensation creeping through her veins, and tingling, half painfully, half pleasurably, at her heart. Still, whenever she dared to look into the mirror, there she beheld herself pale as a white rose and with the crimson birthmark stamped upon her cheek. Not even Aylmer now hated it so much as she.

To dispel the tedium of the hours which her husband found it necessary to devote to the processes of combination and analysis, Georgiana turned over the volumes of his scientific library. In many dark old tomes she met with chapters full of romance and poetry. They were the works of philosophers of the middle ages, such as Albertus Magnus, Cornelius Agrippa, Paracelsus, and the famous friar who created the prophetic Brazen Head. All these antique naturalists stood in advance of their centuries, yet were imbued with some of their credulity, and therefore were believed, and perhaps imagined themselves to have acquired from the investigation of nature a power above nature, and from physics a sway over the spiritual world. Hardly less curious and imaginative were the early volumes of the Transactions of the Royal Society, in which the members, knowing little of the limits of natural possibility, were continually recording wonders or proposing methods whereby wonders might be wrought.

But, to Georgiana, the most engrossing volume was a large folio from her husband's own hand, in which he had recorded every experiment of his scientific career, its original aim, the methods adopted for its development, and its final success or failure, with the circumstances to which either event was attributable. The book, in truth, was both the history and emblem of his ardent, ambitious, imaginative, yet practical and laborious life. He handled physical details as if there were nothing beyond them; yet spiritualized them all, and redeemed himself from materialism by his strong and eager aspiration towards the infinite. In his grasp the veriest clod of earth assumed a soul. Georgiana, as she read, reverenced Aylmer and loved him more profoundly than ever, but with a less entire dependence on his judgment than heretofore. Much as he had accomplished, she could not but observe that his most splendid successes were almost invariably failures, if compared with the ideal at which he aimed. His brightest diamonds were the merest pebbles, and felt to be so by himself, in comparison with the inestimable gems which lay hidden beyond his reach. The volume, rich with achievements that had won renown for its author, was yet as melancholy a record as ever mortal hand had penned. It was the sad confession and continual exemplification of the shortcomings of the composite man, the spirit burdened with clay and working in matter, and of the despair that assails the higher nature at finding itself so miserably thwarted by the earthly part. Perhaps every man of genius, in whatever sphere, might recognize the image of his own experience in Aylmer's journal.

So deeply did these reflections affect Georgiana that she laid her face upon the open volume and burst into tears. In this situation she was found by her husband.

"It is dangerous to read in a sorcerer's books," said he with a smile, though his countenance was uneasy and displeased. "Georgiana, there are pages in that volume which I can scarcely glance over and keep my senses. Take heed lest it prove as detrimental to you."

"It has made me worship you more than ever," said she.

"Ah, wait for this one success," rejoined he, "then worship me if you will. I shall deem myself hardly unworthy of it. But come, I have sought you for the luxury of your voice. Sing to me, dearest."

So she poured out the liquid music of her voice to quench the thirst of his spirit. He then took his leave with a boyish exuberance of gaiety, assuring her that her seclusion would endure but a little longer, and that the result was already certain. Scarcely had he departed when Georgiana felt irresistibly impelled to follow him. She had forgotten to inform Aylmer of a symptom which for two or three hours past had begun to excite her attention. It was a sensation in the fatal birthmark, not painful, but which induced a restlessness throughout her system. Hastening after her husband, she intruded for the first time into the laboratory.

The first thing that struck her eye was the furnace, that hot and feverish worker, with the intense glow of its fire, which by the quantities of soot clustered above it seemed to have been burning for ages. There was a distilling-apparatus in full operation. Around the room were retorts, tubes, cylinders, crucibles, and other apparatus of chemical research. An electrical machine stood ready for immediate use. The atmosphere felt oppressively close, and was tainted with gaseous odors which had been tormented forth by the processes of science. The severe and homely simplicity of the apartment, with its naked walls and brick pavement, looked strange, accustomed as Georgiana had become to the fantastic elegance of her boudoir. But what chiefly, indeed almost solely, drew her attention, was the aspect of Aylmer himself.

He was pale as death, anxious and absorbed, and hung over the furnace as if it depended upon his utmost watchfulness, whether the liquid which it was distilling should be the draught of immortal happiness or misery. How different from the sanguine and joyous mien that he had assumed for Georgiana's encouragement!

"Carefully now, Aminadab; carefully, thou human machine; carefully, thou man of clay!" muttered Aylmer, more to himself than his assistant. "Now, if there be a thought too much or too little, it is all over."

"Ho! ho!" mumbled Aminadab. "Look, master! look!"

Aylmer raised his eyes hastily, and at first reddened, then grew paler than ever, on beholding Georgiana. He rushed towards her and seized her arm with a gripe that left the print of his fingers upon it.

"Why do you come hither? Have you no trust in your husband?" cried he, impetuously. "Would you throw the blight of that fatal birthmark over my labors? It is not well done. Go, prying woman, go!"

"Nay, Aylmer," said Georgiana with the firmness of which she possessed no stinted endowment, "it is not you that have a right to complain. You mistrust your wife; you have concealed the anxiety with which you watch the development of this experiment. Think not so unworthily of me, my husband. Tell me all the risk we run, and fear not that I shall shrink; for my share in it is far less than your own."

"No, no, Georgiana!" said Aylmer, impatiently; "it must not be."

"I submit," replied she, calmly. "And, Aylmer, I shall quaff whatever draught you bring me; but it will be on the same principle that would induce me to take a dose of poison if offered by your hand."

"My noble wife," said Aylmer, deeply moved, "I knew not the height and depth of your nature until now. Nothing shall be concealed. Know, then, that this crimson hand, superficial as it seems, has clutched its grasp into your being with a strength of which I had no previous conception. I have already administered agents powerful enough to do aught except to change your entire physical system. Only one thing remains to be tried. If that fail us we are ruined."

"Why did you hesitate to tell me this?" asked she.

"Because, Georgiana," said Aylmer, in a low voice, "there is danger."

"Danger? There is but one danger – that this horrible stigma shall be left upon my cheek!" cried Georgiana. "Remove it, remove it, whatever be the cost, or we shall both go mad!"

"Heaven knows your words are too true," said Aylmer, sadly. "And now, dearest, return to your boudoir. In a little while all will be tested."

He conducted her back and took leave of her with a solemn tenderness which spoke far more than his words how much was now at stake. After his departure Georgiana became rapt in musings. She considered the character of Aylmer, and did it completer justice than at any previous moment. Her heart exulted, while it trembled, at his honorable love – so pure and lofty that it would accept nothing less than perfection, nor miserably make itself contented with an earthlier nature than he had dreamed of. She felt how much more precious was such a sentiment than that meaner kind which would have borne with the imperfection for her sake, and have been guilty of treason to holy love by degrading its perfect idea to the level of the actual; and with her whole spirit she prayed that, for a single moment, she might satisfy his highest and deepest conception. Longer than one moment she well knew it could not be; for his spirit was ever on the march, ever ascending, and each instant required something that was beyond the scope of the instant before.

The sound of her husband's footsteps aroused her. He bore a crystal goblet containing a liquor colorless as water, but bright enough to be the draught of immortality. Aylmer was pale; but it seemed rather the consequence of a highly wrought state of mind and tension of spirit than of fear or doubt.

"The concoction of the draught has been perfect," said he, in answer to Georgiana's look. "Unless all my science have deceived me, it cannot fail."

"Save on your account, my dearest Aylmer," observed his wife, "I might wish to put off this birthmark of mortality by relinquishing mortality itself in preference to any other mode. Life is but a sad possession to those who have attained precisely the degree of moral advancement at which I stand. Were I weaker and blinder, it might be happiness. Were I stronger, it might be endured hopefully.

But, being what I find myself, methinks I am of all mortals the most fit to die."

"You are fit for heaven without tasting death!" replied her husband. "But why do we speak of dying? The draught cannot fail. Behold its effect upon this plant."

On the window seat there stood a geranium diseased with yellow blotches, which had overspread all its leaves. Aylmer poured a small quantity of the liquid upon the soil in which it grew. In a little time, when the roots of the plant had taken up the moisture, the unsightly blotches began to be extinguished in a living verdure.

"There needed no proof," said Georgiana, quietly. "Give me the goblet. I joyfully stake all upon your word."

"Drink, then, thou lofty creature!" exclaimed Aylmer, with fervid admiration. "There is no taint of imperfection on thy spirit. Thy sensible frame, too, shall soon be all perfect."

She quaffed the liquid and returned the goblet to his hand.

"It is grateful," said she, with a placid smile. "Methinks it is like water from a heavenly fountain; for it contains I know not what of unobtrusive fragrance and deliciousness. It allays a feverish thirst that had parched me for many days. Now, dearest, let me sleep. My earthly senses are closing over my spirit like the leaves around the heart of a rose at sunset."

She spoke the last words with a gentle reluctance, as if it required almost more energy than she could command to pronounce the faint and lingering syllables. Scarcely had they loitered through her lips ere she was lost in slumber.

Aylmer sat by her side, watching her aspect with the emotions proper to a man, the whole value of whose existence was involved in the process now to be tested. Mingled with this mood, however, was the philosophic investigation characteristic of the man of science. Not the minutest symptom escaped him. A heightened flush of the cheek, a slight irregularity of breath, a quiver of the eyelid, a hardly perceptible tremor through the frame, such were the details which, as the moments passed, he wrote down in his folio volume. Intense thought had set its stamp upon every previous page of that volume; but the thoughts of years were all concentrated upon the last.

While thus employed, he failed not to gaze often at the fatal hand, and not without a shudder. Yet once, by a strange and unaccountable impulse he pressed it with his lips. His spirit recoiled, however, in the very act; and Georgiana, out of the midst of her deep sleep, moved uneasily and murmured, as if in remonstrance. Again Aylmer resumed his watch. Nor was it without avail. The crimson hand, which at first had been strongly visible upon the marble paleness of Georgiana's cheek, now grew more faintly outlined. She remained not less pale than ever; but the birthmark with every breath that came and went, lost somewhat of its former distinctness. Its presence had been awful; its departure was more awful still. Watch the stain of the rainbow fading out the sky, and you will know how that mysterious symbol passed away.

"By Heaven! it is well nigh gone!" said Aylmer to himself, in almost irrepressible ecstasy. "I can scarcely trace it now. Success! success! And now it is like the faintest rose color. The lightest flush of blood across her cheek would overcome it. But she is so pale!"

He drew aside the window-curtain and suffered the light of natural day to fall into the room and rest upon her cheek. At the same time he heard a gross, hoarse chuckle, which he had long known as his servant Aminadab's expression of delight.

"Ah, clod! ah, earthly mass!" cried Aylmer, laughing in a sort of frenzy, "you have served me well! Matter and spirit – earth and heaven – have both done their part in this! Laugh, thing of the senses! You have earned the right to laugh."

These exclamations broke Georgiana's sleep. She slowly unclosed her eyes and gazed into the mirror which her husband had arranged for that purpose. A faint smile flitted over her lips when she recognized how barely perceptible was now that crimson hand which had once blazed forth with such disastrous brilliancy as to scare away all their happiness. But then her eyes sought Aylmer's face with a trouble and anxiety that he could by no means account for.

"My poor Aylmer!" murmured she.

"Poor? Nay, richest, happiest, most favored!" exclaimed he. "My peerless bride, it is successful! You are perfect!"

"My poor Aylmer," she repeated, with a more than human tenderness, "you have aimed loftily; you have done nobly. Do not repent that, with so high and pure a feeling, you have rejected the best the earth could offer. Aylmer, dearest Aylmer, I am dying!"

Alas! it was too true! The fatal hand had grappled with the mystery of life, and was the bond by which an angelic spirit kept itself in union with a mortal frame. As the last crimson tint of the birthmark – that sole token of human imperfection – faded from her cheek, the parting breath of the now perfect woman passed into the atmosphere, and her soul, lingering a moment near her husband, took its heavenward flight. Then a hoarse, chuckling laugh was heard again! Thus ever does the gross fatality of earth exult in its invariable triumph over the immortal essence which, in this dim sphere of half-development, demands the completeness of a higher state. Yet, had Alymer reached a profounder wisdom, he need not thus have flung away the happiness which would have woven his mortal life of the self-same texture with the celestial. The momentary circumstance was too strong for him; he failed to look beyond the shadowy scope of time, and, living once for all in eternity, to find the perfect future in the present.

Rappaccini's Daughter

Nathaniel Hawthorne

Introduction

Nathaniel Hawthorne's written works often have a feel of dark romanticism, and *Rappaccini's Daughter* (1844), like *The Birthmark* published the previous year, is a cautionary tale, warning of the darker side of science, showing how tampering with nature can have deadly consequences.

Rappaccini's Daughter

Nathaniel Hawthorne

A young man, named Giovanni Guasconti, came, very long ago, from the more southern region of Italy, to pursue his studies at the University of Padua. Giovanni, who had but a scanty supply of gold ducats in his pocket, took lodgings in a high and gloomy chamber of an old edifice, which looked not unworthy to have been the palace of a Paduan noble, and which, in fact, exhibited over its entrance the armorial bearings of a family long since extinct. The young stranger, who was not unstudied in the great poem of his country, recollected that one of the ancestors of this family, and perhaps an occupant of this very mansion, had been pictured by Dante as a partaker of the immortal agonies of his Inferno. These reminiscences and associations, together with the tendency to heart-break natural to a young man for the first time out of his native sphere, caused Giovanni to sigh heavily, as he looked around the desolate and ill-furnished apartment.

"Holy Virgin, signor," cried old dame Lisabetta, who, won by the youth's remarkable beauty of person, was kindly endeavoring to give the chamber a habitable air, "what a sigh was that to come out of a young man's heart! Do you find this old mansion gloomy? For the love of heaven, then, put your head out of the window, and you will see as bright sunshine as you have left in Naples."

Guasconti mechanically did as the old woman advised, but could not quite agree with her that the Lombard sunshine was as cheerful as that of southern Italy. Such as it was, however, it fell upon a garden beneath the window, and expended its fostering influences on a variety of plants, which seemed to have been cultivated with exceeding care.

"Does this garden belong to the house?" asked Giovanni.

"Heaven forbid, signor!– unless it were fruitful of better pot-herbs than any that grow there now," answered old Lisabetta. "No; that garden is cultivated by the own hands of Signor Giacomo Rappaccini, the famous Doctor, who, I warrant him, has been heard of as far as Naples. It is said he distils these plants into medicines that are as potent as a charm. Oftentimes you may see the Signor Doctor at work, and perchance the Signora his daughter, too, gathering the strange flowers that grow in the garden."

The old woman had now done what she could for the aspect of the chamber, and, commending the young man to the protection of the saints, took her departure.

Giovanni still found no better occupation than to look down into the garden beneath his window. From its appearance, he judged it to be one of those botanic gardens, which were of earlier date in Padua than elsewhere in Italy, or in the world. Or, not improbably, it might once have been the pleasure-place of an opulent family; for there was the ruin of a marble fountain in the center, sculptured with rare art, but so woefully shattered that it was impossible to trace the original design from the chaos of remaining fragments. The water, however, continued to gush and sparkle into the sunbeams as cheerfully as ever. A little gurgling sound ascended to the young man's window, and made him feel as if a fountain were an immortal spirit, that sung its song unceasingly, and without heeding the vicissitudes around it; while one century embodied it in marble, and another scattered the perishable garniture on the soil. All about the pool into which the water subsided, grew various plants, that seemed to require a plentiful supply of moisture for the nourishment of gigantic leaves, and, in some instances, flowers gorgeously magnificent. There was one shrub in particular, set in a marble vase in the midst of the pool, that bore a profusion of purple blossoms, each of which had the luster and richness of a gem; and the whole together made a show so resplendent that it seemed enough to illuminate the garden, even had there been no sunshine. Every portion of the soil was peopled with plants and herbs, which, if less beautiful, still bore tokens of assiduous care; as if all had their individual virtues, known to the scientific mind that fostered them. Some were placed in urns, rich with old carving, and others in common garden-pots; some crept serpent-like along the ground, or climbed on high, using whatever means of ascent was offered them. One plant had wreathed itself round a statue of Vertumnus, which was thus quite veiled and shrouded in a drapery of hanging foliage, so happily arranged that it might have served a sculptor for a study.

While Giovanni stood at the window, he heard a rustling behind a screen of leaves, and became aware that a person was at work in the garden. His figure soon emerged into view, and showed itself to be that of no common laborer, but a tall, emaciated, sallow, and sickly looking man, dressed in a scholar's garb of black. He was beyond the middle term of life, with gray hair, a thin gray beard, and a face singularly marked with intellect and cultivation, but which could never, even in his more youthful days, have expressed much warmth of heart.

Nothing could exceed the intentness with which this scientific gardener examined every shrub which grew in his path; it seemed as if he was looking into their inmost nature, making observations in regard to their creative essence, and discovering why one leaf grew in this shape, and another in that, and wherefore such and such flowers differed among themselves in hue and perfume. Nevertheless, in spite of the deep intelligence on his part, there was no approach to intimacy between himself and these vegetable existences. On the contrary, he avoided their actual touch, or the direct inhaling of their odors, with a caution that impressed Giovanni most disagreeably; for the man's demeanor was that of one walking among malignant influences, such as savage beasts, or deadly snakes, or evil spirits, which, should he allow them one moment of license, would wreak upon him some terrible fatality. It was strangely frightful to the young man's imagination, to see this air of insecurity in a person cultivating a garden, that most simple and innocent of human toils, and which had been alike the joy and labor of the unfallen parents of the race. Was this garden, then, the Eden of the present world?– and this man, with such a perception of harm in what his own hands caused to grow, was he the Adam?

The distrustful gardener, while plucking away the dead leaves or pruning the too luxuriant growth of the shrubs, defended his hands with a pair of thick gloves. Nor were these his only armor. When, in his walk through the garden, he came to the magnificent plant that hung its purple gems beside the marble fountain, he placed a kind of mask over his mouth and nostrils, as if all this beauty did but conceal a deadlier malice. But finding his task still too dangerous, he drew back, removed the mask, and called loudly, but in the infirm voice of a person affected with inward disease:

"Beatrice!– Beatrice!"

"Here am I, my father! What would you?" cried a rich and youthful voice from the window of the opposite house; a voice as rich as a tropical sunset, and which made Giovanni, though he knew not why, think of deep hues of purple or crimson, and of perfumes heavily delectable.– "Are you in the garden?"

"Yes, Beatrice," answered the gardener, "and I need your help."

Soon there emerged from under a sculptured portal the figure of a young girl, arrayed with as much richness of taste as the most splendid of the flowers, beautiful as the day, and with a bloom so deep and vivid that one shade more would have been too much. She looked redundant with life, health, and energy; all of which attributes were bound down and compressed, as it were, and girdled tensely, in their luxuriance, by her virgin zone. Yet Giovanni's fancy must have grown morbid, while he looked down into the garden; for the impression which the fair stranger made upon him was as if here were another flower, the human sister of those vegetable ones, as beautiful as they – more beautiful than the richest of them – but still to be touched only with a glove, nor to be approached without a mask. As Beatrice came down the garden-path, it was observable that she handled and inhaled the odor of several of the plants, which her father had most sedulously avoided.

"Here, Beatrice," said the latter,– "see how many needful offices require to be done to our chief treasure. Yet, shattered as I am, my life might pay the penalty of approaching it so closely as circumstances demand. Henceforth, I fear, this plant must be consigned to your sole charge."

"And gladly will I undertake it," cried again the rich tones of the young lady, as she bent towards the magnificent plant, and opened her arms as if to embrace it. "Yes, my sister, my splendor, it shall be Beatrice's task to nurse and serve thee; and thou shalt reward her with thy kisses and perfume breath, which to her is as the breath of life!"

Then, with all the tenderness in her manner that was so strikingly expressed in her words, she busied herself with such attentions as the plant seemed to require; and Giovanni, at his lofty window, rubbed his eyes, and almost doubted whether it were a girl tending her favorite flower, or one sister performing the duties of affection to another. The scene soon terminated. Whether Doctor Rappaccini had finished his labors in the garden, or that his watchful eye had caught the stranger's face, he now took his daughter's arm and retired. Night was already closing in;

oppressive exhalations seemed to proceed from the plants, and steal upward past the open window; and Giovanni, closing the lattice, went to his couch, and dreamed of a rich flower and beautiful girl. Flower and maiden were different and yet the same, and fraught with some strange peril in either shape.

But there is an influence in the light of morning that tends to rectify whatever errors of fancy, or even of judgment, we may have incurred during the sun's decline, or among the shadows of the night, or in the less wholesome glow of moonshine. Giovanni's first movement on starting from sleep, was to throw open the window, and gaze down into the garden which his dreams had made so fertile of mysteries. He was surprised, and a little ashamed, to find how real and matter-of-fact an affair it proved to be, in the first rays of the sun, which gilded the dew-drops that hung upon leaf and blossom, and, while giving a brighter beauty to each rare flower, brought everything within the limits of ordinary experience. The young man rejoiced, that, in the heart of the barren city, he had the privilege of overlooking this spot of lovely and luxuriant vegetation. It would serve, he said to himself, as a symbolic language, to keep him in communion with Nature. Neither the sickly and thought-worn Doctor Giacomo Rappaccini, it is true, nor his brilliant daughter, were now visible; so that Giovanni could not determine how much of the singularity which he attributed to both, was due to their own qualities, and how much to his wonder-working fancy. But he was inclined to take a most rational view of the whole matter.

In the course of the day, he paid his respects to Signor

Pietro Baglioni, Professor of Medicine in the University, a physician of eminent repute, to whom Giovanni had brought a letter of introduction. The Professor was an elderly personage, apparently of genial nature, and habits that might almost be called jovial; he kept the young man to dinner, and made himself very agreeable by the freedom and liveliness of his conversation, especially when warmed by a flask or two of Tuscan wine. Giovanni, conceiving that men of science, inhabitants of the same city, must needs be on familiar terms with one another, took an opportunity to mention the name of Doctor Rappaccini. But the Professor did not respond with so much cordiality as he had anticipated.

"Ill would it become a teacher of the divine art of medicine," said Professor Pietro Baglioni, in answer to a question of Giovanni, "to withhold due and well-considered praise of a physician so eminently skilled as Rappaccini. But, on the other hand, I should answer it but scantily to my conscience, were I to permit a worthy youth like yourself, Signor Giovanni, the son of an ancient friend, to imbibe erroneous ideas respecting a man who might hereafter chance to hold your life and death in his hands. The truth is, our worshipful Doctor Rappaccini has as much science as any member of the faculty-with perhaps one single exception – in Padua, or all Italy. But there are certain grave objections to his professional character."

"And what are they?" asked the young man.

"Has my friend Giovanni any disease of body or heart, that he is so inquisitive about physicians?" said the Professor, with a smile. "But as for Rappaccini, it is said of him – and I, who know the man well, can answer for its truth – that he cares infinitely more for science than for mankind. His patients are interesting to him only as subjects for some new experiment. He would sacrifice human life, his own among the rest, or whatever else was dearest to him, for the sake of adding so much as a grain of mustard-seed to the great heap of his accumulated knowledge."

"Methinks he is an awful man, indeed," remarked Guasconti, mentally recalling the cold and purely intellectual aspect of Rappaccini. "And yet, worshipful Professor, is it not a noble spirit? Are there many men capable of so spiritual a love of science?"

"God forbid," answered the Professor, somewhat testily – "at least, unless they take sounder views of the healing art than those adopted by Rappaccini. It is his theory, that all medicinal virtues are comprised within those substances which we term vegetable poisons. These he cultivates with his own hands, and is said even to have produced new varieties of poison, more horribly deleterious than Nature, without the assistance of this learned person, would ever have plagued the world withal. That the Signor Doctor does less mischief than might be expected, with such dangerous substances, is undeniable. Now and then, it must be owned, he has effected – or seemed to effect – a marvelous cure. But, to tell you my private mind, Signor Giovanni, he should receive little credit for such instances of success – they being probably the work of chance – but should be held strictly accountable for his failures, which may justly be considered his own work."

The youth might have taken Baglioni's opinions with many grains of allowance, had he known that there was a professional warfare of long continuance between him and Doctor Rappaccini, in which the latter was generally thought to have gained the advantage. If the reader be inclined to judge for himself, we refer him to certain black-letter tracts on both sides, preserved in the medical department of the University of Padua.

"I know not, most learned Professor," returned Giovanni, after musing on what had been said of Rappaccini's exclusive zeal for science – "I know not how dearly this physician may love his art; but surely there is one object more dear to him. He has a daughter."

"Aha!" cried the Professor with a laugh. "So now our friend Giovanni's secret is out. You have heard of this daughter, whom all the young men in Padua are wild about, though not half a dozen have ever had the good hap to see her face. I know little of the Signora Beatrice, save that Rappaccini is said to have instructed her deeply in his science, and that, young and beautiful as fame reports her, she is already qualified to fill a professor's chair. Perchance her father destines her for mine! Other absurd rumors there be, not worth talking about, or listening to. So now, Signor Giovanni, drink off your glass of Lacryma."

Guasconti returned to his lodgings somewhat heated with the wine he had quaffed, and which caused his brain to swim with strange fantasies in reference to Doctor Rappaccini and the beautiful Beatrice. On his way, happening to pass by a florist's, he bought a fresh bouquet of flowers.

Ascending to his chamber, he seated himself near the window, but within the shadow thrown by the depth of the wall, so that he could look down into the garden with little risk of being discovered. All beneath his eye was a solitude. The strange plants were basking in the sunshine, and now and then nodding gently to one another, as if in acknowledgment of sympathy and kindred. In the midst, by the shattered fountain, grew the magnificent shrub, with its purple gems clustering all over it; they glowed in the air, and gleamed back again out of the depths of the pool, which thus seemed to overflow with colored radiance from the rich reflection that was steeped in it. At first, as we have said, the garden was a solitude. Soon, however,– as Giovanni had half hoped, half feared, would be the case,– a figure appeared beneath the antique sculptured portal, and came down between the rows of plants, inhaling their various perfumes, as if she were one of those beings of old classic fable, that lived upon sweet odors. On again beholding Beatrice, the young man was even startled to perceive how much her beauty exceeded his recollection of it; so brilliant, so vivid in its character, that she glowed amid the sunlight, and, as Giovanni whispered to himself, positively illuminated the more shadowy intervals of the garden path. Her face being now more revealed than on the former occasion, he was struck by its expression of simplicity and sweetness; qualities that had not entered into his idea of her character, and which made him ask anew, what manner of mortal she might be. Nor did he fail again to observe, or imagine, an analogy between the beautiful girl and the gorgeous shrub that hung its gem-like flowers over the fountain; a resemblance which Beatrice seemed to have indulged a fantastic humor in heightening, both by the arrangement of her dress and the selection of its hues.

Approaching the shrub, she threw open her arms, as with a passionate ardor, and drew its branches into an intimate embrace; so intimate, that her features were hidden in its leafy bosom, and her glistening ringlets all intermingled with the flowers.

"Give me thy breath, my sister," exclaimed Beatrice; "for I am faint with common air! And give me this flower of thine, which I separate with gentlest fingers from the stem, and place it close beside my heart."

With these words, the beautiful daughter of Rappaccini plucked one of the richest blossoms of the shrub, and was about to fasten it in her bosom. But now, unless Giovanni's draughts of wine had bewildered his senses, a singular incident occurred. A small orange colored reptile, of the lizard or chameleon species, chanced to be creeping along the path, just at the feet of Beatrice. It appeared to Giovanni – but, at the distance from which he gazed, he could scarcely have seen anything so minute – it appeared to him, however, that a drop or two of moisture from the broken stem of the flower descended upon the lizard's head. For an instant, the reptile contorted itself violently, and then lay motionless in the sunshine. Beatrice observed this remarkable phenomenon, and crossed herself, sadly, but without surprise; nor did she therefore hesitate to arrange the fatal flower in her bosom. There it blushed, and almost glimmered with the dazzling effect of a precious stone, adding to her dress and aspect the one appropriate charm, which nothing else in the world could have supplied. But Giovanni, out of the shadow of his window, bent forward and shrank back, and murmured and trembled.

"Am I awake? Have I my senses?" said he to himself. "What is this being?– beautiful, shall I call her?– or inexpressibly terrible?"

Beatrice now strayed carelessly through the garden, approaching closer beneath Giovanni's window, so that he was compelled to thrust his head quite out of its concealment, in order to gratify the intense and painful curiosity which she excited. At this moment, there came a beautiful insect over the garden wall; it had perhaps wandered through the city and found no flowers nor verdure among those antique haunts of men, until the heavy perfumes of Doctor Rappaccini's shrubs had lured it from afar. Without alighting on the flowers, this winged brightness seemed to be attracted by Beatrice, and lingered in the air and fluttered about her head. Now here it could not be but that Giovanni Guasconti's eyes deceived him. Be that as it might, he fancied that while Beatrice was gazing at the insect with childish delight, it grew faint and fell at her feet;– its bright wings shivered; it was dead – from no cause that he could discern, unless it were the atmosphere of her breath. Again Beatrice crossed herself and sighed heavily, as she bent over the dead insect.

An impulsive movement of Giovanni drew her eyes to the window. There she beheld the beautiful head of the young man – rather a Grecian than an Italian head, with fair, regular features, and a glistening of gold among his ringlets – gazing down upon her like a being that hovered in mid-air. Scarcely knowing what he did, Giovanni threw down the bouquet which he had hitherto held in his hand.

"Signora," said he, "there are pure and healthful flowers. Wear them for the sake of Giovanni Guasconti!"

"Thanks, Signor," replied Beatrice, with her rich voice that came forth as it were like a gush of music; and with a mirthful expression half childish and half woman-like. "I accept your gift, and would fain recompense it with this precious purple flower; but if I toss it into the air, it will not reach you. So Signor Guasconti must even content himself with my thanks."

She lifted the bouquet from the ground, and then as if inwardly ashamed at having stepped aside from her maidenly reserve to respond to a stranger's greeting, passed swiftly homeward through the garden. But, few as the moments were, it seemed to Giovanni when she was on the point of vanishing beneath the sculptured portal, that his beautiful bouquet was already beginning to wither in her grasp. It was an idle thought; there could be no possibility of distinguishing a faded flower from a fresh one, at so great a distance.

For many days after this incident, the young man avoided the window that looked into Doctor Rappaccini's garden, as if something ugly and monstrous would have blasted his eye-sight, had he been betrayed into a glance. He felt conscious of having put himself, to a certain extent, within the influence of an unintelligible power, by the communication which he had opened with Beatrice. The wisest course would have been, if his heart were in any real danger, to quit his lodgings and Padua itself, at once; the next wiser, to have accustomed himself, as far as possible, to the familiar and day-light view of Beatrice; thus bringing her rigidly and systematically within the limits of ordinary experience. Least of all, while avoiding her sight, should Giovanni have remained so near this extraordinary being, that the proximity and possibility even of intercourse, should give a kind of substance and reality to the wild vagaries which his imagination ran riot continually in producing. Guasconti had not a deep heart – or at all events, its depths were not sounded now – but he had a quick fancy, and an ardent southern temperament, which rose every instant to a higher fever-pitch. Whether or no Beatrice possessed those terrible attributes – that fatal breath – the affinity with those so beautiful and deadly flowers – which were indicated by what Giovanni had witnessed, she had at least instilled a fierce and subtle poison into his system. It was not love, although her rich beauty was a madness to him; nor horror, even while he fancied her spirit to be imbued with the same baneful essence that seemed to pervade her physical frame; but a wild offspring of both love and horror that had each parent in it, and burned like one and shivered like the other. Giovanni knew not what to dread; still less did he know what to hope; yet hope and dread kept a continual warfare in his breast, alternately vanquishing one another and starting up afresh to renew the contest. Blessed are all simple emotions, be they dark or bright! It is the lurid intermixture of the two that produces the illuminating blaze of the infernal regions. Sometimes he endeavored to assuage the fever of his spirit by a rapid walk through the streets of Padua, or beyond its gates; his footsteps kept time with the throbbings of his brain, so that the walk was apt to accelerate itself to a race. One day, he found himself arrested; his arm was seized by a portly personage who had turned back on recognizing the young man, and expended much breath in overtaking him.

"Signor Giovanni!– stay, my young friend!"– cried he. "Have you forgotten me? That might well be the case, if I were as much altered as yourself."

It was Baglioni, whom Giovanni had avoided, ever since their first meeting, from a doubt that the Professor's sagacity would look too deeply into his secrets. Endeavoring to recover himself, he stared forth wildly from his inner world into the outer one, and spoke like a man in a dream.

"Yes; I am Giovanni Guasconti. You are Professor Pietro Baglioni. Now let me pass!"

"Not yet – not yet, Signor Giovanni Guasconti," said the Professor, smiling, but at the same time scrutinizing the youth with an earnest glance. "What, did I grow up side by side with your father, and shall his son pass me like a stranger, in these old streets of Padua? Stand still, Signor Giovanni; for we must have a word or two before we part."

"Speedily, then, most worshipful Professor, speedily!" said Giovanni, with feverish impatience. "Does not your worship see that I am in haste?"

Now, while he was speaking, there came a man in black along the street, stooping and moving feebly, like a person in inferior health. His face was all overspread with a most sickly and sallow hue, but yet so pervaded with an expression of piercing and active intellect, that an observer might easily have overlooked the merely physical attributes, and have seen only this wonderful energy. As he passed, this person exchanged a cold and distant salutation with Baglioni, but fixed his eyes upon Giovanni with an intentness that seemed to bring out whatever was within him worthy of notice. Nevertheless, there was a peculiar quietness in the look, as if taking merely a speculative, not a human interest, in the young man.

"It is Doctor Rappaccini!" whispered the Professor, when the stranger had passed.– "Has he ever seen your face before?"

"Not that I know," answered Giovanni, starting at the name.

"He has seen you!– he must have seen you!" said Baglioni, hastily. "For some purpose or other, this man of science is making a study of you. I know that look of his! It is the same that coldly illuminates his face, as he bends over a bird, a mouse, or a butterfly, which, in pursuance of some experiment, he has killed by the perfume of a flower;– a look as deep as Nature itself, but without Nature's warmth of love. Signor Giovanni, I will stake my life upon it, you are the subject of one of Rappaccini's experiments!"

"Will you make a fool of me?" cried Giovanni, passionately. "That, Signor Professor, were an untoward experiment."

"Patience, patience!" replied the imperturbable Professor. "I tell thee, my poor Giovanni, that Rappaccini has a scientific interest in thee. Thou hast fallen into fearful hands! And the Signora Beatrice? What part does she act in this mystery?"

But Guasconti, finding Baglioni's pertinacity intolerable, here broke away, and was gone before the Professor could again seize his arm. He looked after the young man intently, and shook his head.

"This must not be," said Baglioni to himself. "The youth is the son of my old friend, and shall not come to any harm from which the arcana of medical science can preserve him. Besides, it is too insufferable an impertinence in Rappaccini thus to snatch the lad out of my own hands, as I may say, and make use of him for his infernal experiments. This daughter of his! It shall be looked to. Perchance, most learned Rappaccini, I may foil you where you little dream of it!"

Meanwhile, Giovanni had pursued a circuitous route, and at length found himself at the door of his lodgings. As he crossed the threshold, he was met by old Lisabetta, who smirked and smiled, and was evidently desirous to attract his attention; vainly, however, as the ebullition of his feelings had momentarily subsided into a cold and dull vacuity. He turned his eyes full upon the withered face that was puckering itself into a smile, but seemed to behold it not. The old dame, therefore, laid her grasp upon his cloak.

"Signor!– Signor!" whispered she, still with a smile over the whole breadth of her visage, so that it looked not unlike a grotesque carving in wood, darkened by centuries – "Listen, Signor! There is a private entrance into the garden!"

"What do you say?" exclaimed Giovanni, turning quickly

about, as if an inanimate thing should start into feverish life.– "A private entrance into Doctor Rappaccini's garden!"

"Hush! Hush!– not so loud!" whispered Lisabetta, putting her hand over his mouth. "Yes; into the worshipful Doctor's garden, where you may see all his fine shrubbery. Many a young man in Padua would give gold to be admitted among those flowers."

Giovanni put a piece of gold into her hand.

"Show me the way," said he.

A surmise, probably excited by his conversation with Baglioni, crossed his mind, that this interposition of old Lisabetta might perchance be connected with the intrigue, whatever were its nature, in which the Professor seemed to suppose that Doctor Rappaccini was involving him. But such a suspicion, though it disturbed Giovanni, was inadequate to restrain him. The instant he was aware of the possibility of approaching Beatrice, it seemed an absolute necessity of his existence to do so. It mattered not whether she were angel or demon; he was irrevocably within her sphere, and must obey the law that whirled him onward, in ever lessening circles, towards a result which he did not attempt to foreshadow. And yet, strange to say, there came across him a sudden doubt, whether this intense interest on his part were not delusory – whether it were really of so deep and positive a nature as to justify him in now thrusting himself into an incalculable position – whether it were not merely the fantasy of a young man's brain, only slightly, or not at all, connected with his heart!

He paused – hesitated – turned half about – but again went on. His withered guide led him along several obscure passages, and finally undid a door, through which, as it was opened, there came the sight and sound of rustling leaves, with the broken sunshine glimmering among them. Giovanni stepped forth, and forcing himself through the entanglement of a shrub that wreathed its tendrils over the hidden entrance, he stood beneath his own window, in the open area of Doctor Rappaccini's garden.

How often is it the case, that, when impossibilities have come to pass, and dreams have condensed their misty substance into tangible realities, we find ourselves calm, and even coldly self-possessed, amid circumstances which it would have been a delirium of joy or agony to anticipate! Fate delights to thwart us thus. Passion will choose his own time to rush upon the scene, and lingers sluggishly behind, when an appropriate adjustment of events would seem to summon his appearance. So was it now with Giovanni. Day after day, his pulses had throbbed with feverish blood, at the improbable idea of an interview with Beatrice, and of standing with her, face to face, in this very garden, basking in the oriental sunshine of her beauty, and snatching from her full gaze the mystery which he deemed the riddle of his own existence. But now there was a singular and untimely equanimity within his breast. He threw a glance around the garden to discover if Beatrice or her father were present, and perceiving that he was alone, began a critical observation of the plants.

The aspect of one and all of them dissatisfied him; their gorgeousness seemed fierce, passionate, and even unnatural. There was hardly an individual shrub which a wanderer, straying by himself through a forest, would not have been startled to find growing wild, as if an unearthly face had glared at him out of the thicket. Several, also, would have shocked a delicate instinct by an appearance of artificialness, indicating that there had been such commixture, and, as it were, adultery of various vegetable species, that the production was no longer of God's making, but the monstrous offspring of man's depraved fancy, glowing with only an evil mockery of beauty. They were probably the result of experiment, which, in one or two cases, had succeeded in mingling plants individually lovely into a compound possessing the questionable and ominous character that distinguished the whole growth of the garden. In fine, Giovanni recognized but two or three plants in the collection, and those of a kind that he well knew to be poisonous. While busy with these contemplations, he heard the rustling of a silken garment, and turning, beheld Beatrice emerging from beneath the sculptured portal.

Giovanni had not considered with himself what should be his deportment; whether he should apologize for his intrusion into the garden, or assume that he was there with the privity, at least, if not by the desire, of Doctor Rappaccini or his daughter. But Beatrice's manner placed him at his ease, though leaving him still in doubt by what agency he had gained admittance. She came lightly along the path, and met him near the broken fountain. There was surprise in her face, but brightened by a simple and kind expression of pleasure.

"You are a connoisseur in flowers, Signor," said Beatrice with a smile, alluding to the bouquet which he had flung her from the window. "It is no marvel, therefore, if the sight of my father's rare collection has tempted you to take a nearer view. If he were here, he could tell you many strange and interesting facts as to the nature and habits of these shrubs, for he has spent a life-time in such studies, and this garden is his world."

"And yourself, lady,"– observed Giovanni –"if fame says true – you, likewise, are deeply skilled in the virtues indicated by these rich blossoms, and these spicy perfumes. Would you deign to be my instructress, I should prove an apter scholar than under Signor Rappaccini himself."

"Are there such idle rumors?" asked Beatrice, with the music of a pleasant laugh. "Do people say that I am skilled in my father's science of plants? What a jest is there! No; though I have grown up among these flowers, I know no more of them than their hues and perfume; and sometimes, methinks I would fain rid myself of even that small knowledge. There are many flowers here, and those not the least brilliant, that shock and offend me, when they meet my eye. But, pray, Signor, do not believe these stories about my science. Believe nothing of me save what you see with your own eyes."

"And must I believe all that I have seen with my own eyes?" asked Giovanni pointedly, while the recollection of former scenes made him shrink. "No, Signora, you demand too little of me. Bid me believe nothing, save what comes from your own lips."

It would appear that Beatrice understood him. There came a deep flush to her cheek; but she looked full into Giovanni's eyes, and responded to his gaze of uneasy suspicion with a queen-like haughtiness.

"I do so bid you, Signor!" she replied. "Forget whatever you may have fancied in regard to me. If true to the outward senses, still it may be false in its essence. But the words of Beatrice Rappaccini's lips are true from the heart outward. Those you may believe!"

A fervor glowed in her whole aspect, and beamed upon Giovanni's consciousness like the light of truth itself. But while she spoke, there was a fragrance in the atmosphere around her rich and delightful, though evanescent, yet which the young man, from an indefinable reluctance, scarcely dared to draw into his lungs. It might be the odor of the flowers. Could it be Beatrice's breath, which thus embalmed her words with a strange richness, as if by steeping them in her heart? A faintness passed like a shadow over Giovanni, and flitted away; he seemed to gaze through the beautiful girl's eyes into her transparent soul, and felt no more doubt or fear.

The tinge of passion that had colored Beatrice's manner vanished; she became gay, and appeared to derive a pure delight from her communion with the youth, not unlike what the maiden of a lonely island might have felt, conversing with a voyager from the civilized world. Evidently her experience of life had been confined within the limits of that garden. She talked now about matters as simple as the day-light or summer-clouds, and now asked questions in reference to the city, or Giovanni's distant home, his friends, his mother, and his sisters; questions indicating such seclusion, and such lack of familiarity with modes and forms, that Giovanni responded as if to an infant. Her spirit gushed out before him like a fresh rill, that was just catching its first glimpse of the sunlight, and wondering, at the reflections of earth and sky which were flung into its bosom. There came thoughts, too, from a deep source, and fantasies of a gem-like brilliancy, as if diamonds and rubies sparkled upward among the bubbles of the fountain. Ever and anon, there gleamed across the young man's mind a sense of wonder, that he should be walking side by side with the being who had so wrought upon his imagination – whom he had idealized in such hues of terror – in whom he had positively witnessed such manifestations of dreadful attributes – that he should be conversing with Beatrice like a brother, and should find her so human and so maiden-like. But such reflections were only momentary; the effect of her character was too real, not to make itself familiar at once.

In this free intercourse, they had strayed through the garden, and now, after many turns among its avenues, were come to the shattered fountain, beside which grew the magnificent shrub with its treasury of glowing blossoms.

A fragrance was diffused from it, which Giovanni recognized as identical with that which he had attributed to Beatrice's breath, but incomparably more powerful. As her eyes fell upon it, Giovanni beheld her press her hand to her bosom, as if her heart were throbbing suddenly and painfully.

"For the first time in my life," murmured she, addressing the shrub, "I had forgotten thee!"

"I remember, Signora," said Giovanni, "that you once promised to reward me with one of these living gems for the bouquet, which I had the happy boldness to fling to your feet. Permit me now to pluck it as a memorial of this interview."

He made a step towards the shrub, with extended hand. But Beatrice darted forward, uttering a shriek that went through his heart like a dagger. She caught his hand, and drew it back with the whole force of her slender figure. Giovanni felt her touch thrilling through his fibers.

"Touch it not!" exclaimed she, in a voice of agony. "Not for thy life! It is fatal!"

Then, hiding her face, she fled from him, and vanished beneath the sculptured portal. As Giovanni followed her with his eyes, he beheld the emaciated figure and pale intelligence of Doctor Rappaccini, who had been watching the scene, he knew not how long, within the shadow of the entrance.

No sooner was Guasconti alone in his chamber, than the image of Beatrice came back to his passionate musings, invested with all the witchery that had been gathering around it ever since his first glimpse of her, and now likewise imbued with a tender warmth of girlish womanhood. She was human: her nature was endowed with all gentle and feminine qualities; she was worthiest to be worshipped; she was capable, surely, on her part, of the height and heroism of love. Those tokens, which he had hitherto considered as proofs of a frightful peculiarity in her physical and moral system, were now either forgotten, or, by the subtle sophistry of passion, transmuted into a golden crown of enchantment, rendering Beatrice the more admirable, by so much as she was the more unique. Whatever had looked ugly, was now beautiful; or, if incapable of such a change, it stole away and hid itself among those shapeless half-ideas, which throng the dim region beyond the daylight of our perfect consciousness. Thus did Giovanni spend the night, nor fell asleep, until the dawn had begun to awake the slumbering flowers in Doctor Rappaccini's garden, whither his dreams doubtless led him. Up rose the sun in his due season, and flinging his beams upon the young man's eyelids, awoke him to a sense of pain. When thoroughly aroused, he became sensible of a burning and tingling agony in his hand – in his right hand – the very hand which Beatrice had grasped in her own, when he was on the point of plucking one of the gem-like flowers. On the back of that hand there was now a purple print, like that of four small fingers, and the likeness of a slender thumb upon his wrist.

Oh, how stubbornly does love – or even that cunning semblance of love which flourishes in the imagination, but strikes no depth of root into the heart – how stubbornly does it hold its faith, until the moment comes, when it is doomed to vanish into thin mist! Giovanni wrapt a handkerchief about his hand, and wondered what evil thing had stung him, and soon forgot his pain in a reverie of Beatrice.

After the first interview, a second was in the inevitable course of what we call fate. A third; a fourth; and a meeting with Beatrice in the garden was no longer an incident in Giovanni's daily life, but the whole space in which he might be said to live; for the anticipation and memory of that ecstatic hour made up the remainder. Nor was it otherwise with the daughter of Rappaccini. She watched for the youth's appearance, and flew to his side with confidence as unreserved as if they had been playmates from early infancy – as if they were such playmates still. If, by any unwonted chance, he failed to come at the appointed moment, she stood beneath the window, and sent up the rich sweetness of her tones to float around him in his chamber, and echo and reverberate throughout his heart –"Giovanni! Giovanni! Why tarriest thou? Come down!" And down he hastened into that Eden of poisonous flowers.

But, with all this intimate familiarity, there was still a reserve in Beatrice's demeanor, so rigidly and invariably sustained, that the idea of infringing it scarcely occurred to his imagination. By all appreciable signs, they loved; they had looked love, with eyes that conveyed the holy secret from the depths of one soul into the depths of the other, as if it were too sacred to be whispered by the way; they had even spoken love, in those gushes of passion when their spirits darted forth in articulated breath, like tongues of long-hidden flame; and yet there had been no seal of lips, no clasp of hands, nor any slightest caress, such as love claims and hallows. He had never touched one of the gleaming ringlets of her hair; her garment – so marked was the physical barrier between them – had never been waved against him by a breeze. On the few occasions when Giovanni had seemed tempted to overstep the limit, Beatrice grew so sad, so stern, and withal wore such a look of desolate separation, shuddering at itself, that not a spoken word was requisite to repel him. At such times, he was startled at the horrible suspicions that rose, monster-like, out of the caverns of his heart, and stared him in the face; his love grew thin and faint as the morning-mist; his doubts alone had substance. But when Beatrice's face brightened again, after the momentary shadow, she was transformed at once from the mysterious, questionable being, whom he had watched with so much awe and horror; she was now the beautiful and unsophisticated girl, whom he felt that his spirit knew with a certainty beyond all other knowledge.

A considerable time had now passed since Giovanni's last meeting with Baglioni. One morning, however, he was disagreeably surprised by a visit from the Professor, whom he had scarcely thought of for whole weeks, and would willingly have forgotten still longer. Given up, as he had long been, to a pervading excitement, he could tolerate no companions, except upon condition of their perfect sympathy with his present state of feeling. Such sympathy was not to be expected from Professor Baglioni. The visitor chatted carelessly, for a few moments, about the gossip of the city and the University, and then took up another topic.

"I have been reading an old classic author lately," said he, "and met with a story that strangely interested me. Possibly you may remember it. It is of an Indian prince, who sent a beautiful woman as a present to Alexander the Great. She was as lovely as the dawn, and gorgeous as the sunset; but what especially distinguished her was a certain rich perfume in her breath-richer than a garden of Persian roses. Alexander, as was natural to a youthful conqueror, fell in love at first sight with this magnificent stranger. But a certain sage physician, happening to be present, discovered a terrible secret in regard to her."

"And what was that?" asked Giovanni, turning his eyes downward to avoid those of the Professor.

"That this lovely woman," continued Baglioni, with emphasis, "had been nourished with poisons from her birth upward, until her whole nature was so imbued with them, that she herself had become the deadliest poison in existence. Poison was her element of life. With that rich perfume of her breath, she blasted the very air. Her love would have been poison!– her embrace death! Is not this a marvelous tale?"

"A childish fable," answered Giovanni, nervously starting from his chair. "I marvel how your worship finds time to read such nonsense, among your graver studies."

"By the bye," said the Professor, looking uneasily about him, "what singular fragrance is this in your apartment? Is it the perfume of your gloves? It is faint, but delicious, and yet, after all, by no means agreeable. Were I to breathe it long, methinks it would make me ill. It is like the breath of a flower – but I see no flowers in the chamber."

"Nor are there any," replied Giovanni, who had turned pale as the Professor spoke; "nor, I think, is there any fragrance, except in your worship's imagination. Odors, being a sort of element combined of the sensual and the spiritual, are apt to deceive us in this manner. The recollection of a perfume – the bare idea of it – may easily be mistaken for a present reality."

"Aye; but my sober imagination does not often play such tricks," said Baglioni; "and were I to fancy any kind of odor, it would be that of some vile apothecary drug, wherewith my fingers are likely enough to be imbued. Our worshipful friend Rappaccini, as I have heard, tinctures his medicaments with odors richer than those of Araby. Doubtless, likewise, the fair and learned Signora Beatrice would minister to her patients with draughts as sweet as a maiden's breath. But wo to him that sips them!"

Giovanni's face evinced many contending emotions. The tone in which the Professor alluded to the pure and lovely daughter of Rappaccini was a torture to his soul; and yet, the intimation of a view of her character, opposite to his own, gave instantaneous distinctness to a thousand dim suspicions, which now grinned at him like so many demons. But he strove hard to quell them, and to respond to Baglioni with a true lover's perfect faith.

"Signor Professor," said he, "you were my father's friend – perchance, too, it is your purpose to act a friendly part towards his son. I would fain feel nothing towards you save respect and deference. But I pray you to observe, Signor, that there is one subject on which we must not speak. You know not the Signora Beatrice. You cannot, therefore, estimate the wrong – the blasphemy, I may even say – that is offered to her character by a light or injurious word."

"Giovanni!– my poor Giovanni!" answered the Professor, with a calm expression of pity, "I know this wretched girl far better than yourself. You shall hear the truth in respect to the poisoner Rappaccini, and his poisonous daughter. Yes; poisonous as she is beautiful! Listen; for even should you do violence to my gray hairs, it shall not silence me. That old fable of the Indian woman has become a truth, by the deep and deadly science of Rappaccini, and in the person of the lovely Beatrice!"

Giovanni groaned and hid his face.

"Her father," continued Baglioni, "was not restrained by natural affection from offering up his child, in this horrible manner, as the victim of his insane zeal for science. For – let us do him justice – he is as true a man of science as ever distilled his own heart in an alembic. What, then, will be your fate? Beyond a doubt, you are selected as the material of some new experiment. Perhaps the result is to be death – perhaps a fate more awful still! Rappaccini, with what he calls the interest of science before his eyes, will hesitate at nothing."

"It is a dream!" muttered Giovanni to himself, "surely it is a dream!"

"But," resumed the Professor, "be of good cheer, son of my friend! It is not yet too late for the rescue. Possibly, we may even succeed in bringing back this miserable child within the limits of ordinary nature, from which her father's madness has estranged her. Behold this little silver vase! It was wrought by the hands of the renowned Benvenuto Cellini, and is well worthy to be a love-gift to the fairest dame in Italy. But its contents are invaluable. One little sip of this antidote would have rendered the most virulent poisons of the Borgias innocuous. Doubt not that it will be as efficacious against those of Rappaccini. Bestow the vase, and the precious liquid within it, on your Beatrice, and hopefully await the result."

Baglioni laid a small, exquisitely wrought silver phial on the table, and withdrew, leaving what he had said to produce its effect upon the young man's mind.

"We will thwart Rappaccini yet!" thought he, chuckling

to himself, as he descended the stairs. "But, let us confess the truth of him, he is a wonderful man!– a wonderful man indeed! A vile empiric, however, in his practice, and therefore not to be tolerated by those who respect the good old rules of the medical profession!"

Throughout Giovanni's whole acquaintance with Beatrice, he had occasionally, as we have said, been haunted by dark surmises as to her character. Yet, so thoroughly had she made herself felt by him as a simple, natural, most affectionate and guileless creature, that the image now held up by Professor Baglioni, looked as strange and incredible, as if it were not in accordance with his own original conception. True, there were ugly recollections connected with his first glimpses of the beautiful girl; he could not quite forget the bouquet that withered in her grasp, and the insect that perished amid the sunny air, by no ostensible agency save the fragrance of her breath. These incidents, however, dissolving in the pure light of her character, had no longer the efficacy of facts, but were acknowledged as mistaken fantasies, by whatever testimony of the senses they might appear to be substantiated. There is something truer and more real, than what we can see with the eyes, and touch with the finger. On such better evidence, had Giovanni founded his confidence in Beatrice, though rather by the necessary force of her high attributes, than by any deep and generous faith on his part. But, now, his spirit was incapable of sustaining itself at the height to which the early enthusiasm of passion had exalted it; he fell down, grovelling among earthly doubts, and defiled therewith the pure whiteness of Beatrice's image. Not that he gave her up; he did but distrust. He resolved to institute some decisive test that should satisfy him, once for all, whether there were those dreadful peculiarities in her physical nature, which could not be supposed to exist without some corresponding monstrosity of soul. His eyes, gazing down afar, might have deceived him as to the lizard, the insect, and the flowers. But if he could witness, at the distance of a few paces, the sudden blight of one fresh and healthful flower in Beatrice's hand, there would be room for no further question. With this idea, he hastened to the florist's, and purchased a bouquet that was still gemmed with the morning dew-drops.

It was now the customary hour of his daily interview with Beatrice. Before descending into the garden, Giovanni failed not to look at his figure in the mirror; a vanity to be expected in a beautiful young man, yet, as displaying itself at that troubled and feverish moment, the token of a certain shallowness of feeling and insincerity of character. He did gaze, however, and said to himself, that his features had never before possessed so rich a grace, nor his eyes such vivacity, nor his cheeks so warm a hue of superabundant life.

"At least," thought he, "her poison has not yet insinuated itself into my system. I am no flower to perish in her grasp!"

With that thought, he turned his eyes on the bouquet, which he had never once laid aside from his hand. A thrill of indefinable horror shot through his frame, on perceiving that those dewy flowers were already beginning to droop; they wore the aspect of things that had been fresh and lovely, yesterday. Giovanni grew white as marble, and stood motionless before the mirror, staring at his own reflection there, as at the likeness of something frightful. He remembered Baglioni's remark about the fragrance that seemed to pervade the chamber. It must have been the poison in his breath! Then he shuddered – shuddered at himself! Recovering from his stupor, he began to watch, with curious eye, a spider that was busily at work, hanging its web from the antique cornice of the apartment, crossing and re-crossing the artful system of interwoven lines, as vigorous and active a spider as ever dangled from an old ceiling. Giovanni bent towards the insect, and emitted a deep, long breath. The spider suddenly ceased its toil; the web vibrated with a tremor originating in the body of the small artizan. Again Giovanni sent forth a breath, deeper, longer, and imbued with a venomous feeling out of his heart; he knew not whether he were wicked or only desperate. The spider made a convulsive gripe with his limbs, and hung dead across the window.

"Accursed! Accursed!" muttered Giovanni, addressing himself. "Hast thou grown so poisonous, that this deadly insect perishes by thy breath?"

At that moment, a rich, sweet voice came floating up from the garden: "Giovanni! Giovanni! It is past the hour! Why tarriest thou! Come down!"

"Yes," muttered Giovanni again. "She is the only being whom my breath may not slay! Would that it might!"

He rushed down, and in an instant, was standing before the bright and loving eyes of Beatrice. A moment ago, his wrath and despair had been so fierce that he could have desired nothing so much as to wither her by a glance. But, with her actual presence, there came influences which had too real an existence to be at once shaken off; recollections of the delicate and benign power of her feminine nature, which had so often enveloped him in a religious calm; recollections of many a holy and passionate outgush of her heart, when the pure fountain had been unsealed from its depths, and made visible in its transparency to his mental eye; recollections which, had Giovanni known how to estimate them, would have assured him that all this ugly mystery was but an earthly illusion, and that, whatever mist of evil might seem to have gathered over her, the real Beatrice was a heavenly angel. Incapable as he was of such high faith, still her presence had not utterly lost its magic. Giovanni's rage was quelled into an aspect of sullen insensibility. Beatrice, with a quick spiritual sense, immediately felt that there was a gulf of blackness between them, which neither he nor she could pass. They walked on together, sad and silent, and came thus to the marble fountain, and to its pool of water on the ground, in the midst of which grew the shrub that bore gem-like blossoms. Giovanni was affrighted at the eager enjoyment – the appetite, as it were-with which he found himself inhaling the fragrance of the flowers.

"Beatrice," asked he abruptly, "whence came this shrub!"

"My father created it," answered she, with simplicity.

"Created it! created it!" repeated Giovanni. "What mean you, Beatrice?"

"He is a man fearfully acquainted with the secrets of nature," replied Beatrice; "and, at the hour when I first drew breath, this plant sprang from the soil, the offspring of his science, of his intellect, while I was but his earthly child. Approach it not!" continued she, observing with terror that Giovanni was drawing nearer to the shrub. "It has qualities that you little dream of. But I, dearest Giovanni – I grew up and blossomed with the plant, and was nourished with its breath. It was my sister, and I loved it with a human affection: for – alas! hast thou not suspected it? there was an awful doom."

Here Giovanni frowned so darkly upon her that Beatrice paused and trembled. But her faith in his tenderness reassured her, and made her blush that she had doubted for an instant.

"There was an awful doom," she continued,– "the effect of my father's fatal love of science – which estranged me from all society of my kind. Until Heaven sent thee, dearest Giovanni, Oh! how lonely was thy poor Beatrice!"

"Was it a hard doom?" asked Giovanni, fixing his eyes upon her.

"Only of late have I known how hard it was," answered she tenderly. "Oh, yes; but my heart was torpid, and therefore quiet."

Giovanni's rage broke forth from his sullen gloom like a lightning-flash out of a dark cloud.

"Accursed one!" cried he, with venomous scorn and anger. "And finding thy solitude wearisome, thou hast severed me, likewise, from all the warmth of life, and enticed me into thy region of unspeakable horror!"

"Giovanni!" exclaimed Beatrice, turning her large bright eyes upon his face. The force of his words had not found its way into her mind; she was merely thunder-struck.

"Yes, poisonous thing!" repeated Giovanni, beside himself with passion. "Thou hast done it! Thou hast blasted me! Thou hast filled my veins with poison! Thou hast made me as hateful, as ugly, as loathsome and deadly a creature as thyself – a world's wonder of hideous monstrosity! Now – if our breath be happily as fatal to ourselves as to all others – let us join our lips in one kiss of unutterable hatred, and so die!"

"What has befallen me?" murmured Beatrice, with a low moan out of her heart. "Holy Virgin pity me, a poor heartbroken child!"

"Thou! Dost thou pray?" cried Giovanni, still with the same fiendish scorn. "Thy very prayers, as they come from thy lips, taint the atmosphere with death. Yes, yes; let us pray! Let us to church, and dip our fingers in the holy water at the portal! They that come after us will perish as by a pestilence. Let us sign crosses in the air! It will be scattering curses abroad in the likeness of holy symbols!"

"Giovanni," said Beatrice calmly, for her grief was beyond passion, "Why dost thou join thyself with me thus in those terrible words? I, it is true, am the horrible thing thou namest me. But thou!– what hast thou to do, save with one other shudder at my hideous misery, to go forth out of the garden and mingle with thy race, and forget that there ever crawled on earth such a monster as poor Beatrice?"

"Dost thou pretend ignorance?" asked Giovanni, scowling upon her. "Behold! This power have I gained from the pure daughter of Rappaccini!"

There was a swarm of summer-insects flitting through

the air, in search of the food promised by the flower-odors of the fatal garden. They circled round Giovanni's head, and were evidently attracted towards him by the same influence which had drawn them, for an instant, within the sphere of several of the shrubs. He sent forth a breath among them, and smiled bitterly at Beatrice, as at least a score of the insects fell dead upon the ground.

"I see it! I see it!" shrieked Beatrice. "It is my father's fatal science? No, no, Giovanni; it was not I! Never, never! I dreamed only to love thee, and be with thee a little time, and so to let thee pass away, leaving but thine image in mine heart. For, Giovanni – believe it – though my body be nourished with poison, my spirit is God's creature, and craves love as its daily food. But my father!– he has united us in this fearful sympathy. Yes; spurn me!– tread upon me!– kill me! Oh, what is death, after such words as thine? But it was not I! Not for a world of bliss would I have done it!"

Giovanni's passion had exhausted itself in its outburst from his lips. There now came across him a sense, mournful, and not without tenderness, of the intimate and peculiar relationship between Beatrice and himself. They stood, as it were, in an utter solitude, which would be made none the less solitary by the densest throng of human life. Ought not, then, the desert of humanity around them to press this insulated pair closer together? If they should be cruel to one another, who was there to be kind to them? Besides, thought Giovanni, might there not still be a hope of his returning within the limits of ordinary nature, and leading Beatrice – the redeemed Beatrice – by the hand?

Oh, weak, and selfish, and unworthy spirit, that could dream of an earthly union and earthly happiness as possible, after such deep love had been so bitterly wronged as was Beatrice's love by Giovanni's blighting words! No, no; there could be no such hope. She must pass heavily, with that broken heart, across the borders of Time – she must bathe her hurts in some fount of Paradise, and forget her grief in the light of immortality – and there be well!

But Giovanni did not know it.

"Dear Beatrice," said he, approaching her, while she shrank away, as always at his approach, but now with a different impulse –"dearest Beatrice, our fate is not yet so desperate. Behold! There is a medicine, potent, as a wise physician has assured me, and almost divine in its efficacy. It is composed of ingredients the most opposite to those by which thy awful father has brought this calamity upon thee and me. It is distilled of blessed herbs. Shall we not quaff it together, and thus be purified from evil?"

"Give it me!" said Beatrice, extending her hand to receive the little silver phial which Giovanni took from his bosom. She added, with a peculiar emphasis: "I will drink – but do thou await the result."

She put Baglioni's antidote to her lips; and, at the same moment, the figure of Rappaccini emerged from the portal, and came slowly towards the marble fountain. As he drew near, the pale man of science seemed to gaze with a triumphant expression at the beautiful youth and maiden, as might an artist who should spend his life in achieving a picture or a group of statuary, and finally be satisfied with his success. He paused – his bent form grew erect with conscious power, he spread out his hand over them, in the attitude of a father imploring a blessing upon his children. But those were the same hands that had thrown poison into the stream of their lives! Giovanni trembled. Beatrice shuddered very nervously, and pressed her hand upon her heart.

"My daughter," said Rappaccini, "thou art no longer lonely in the world! Pluck one of those precious gems from thy sister shrub, and bid thy bridegroom wear it in his bosom. It will not harm him now! My science, and the sympathy between thee and him, have so wrought within his system, that he now stands apart from common men, as thou dost, daughter of my pride and triumph, from ordinary women. Pass on, then, through the world, most dear to one another, and dreadful to all besides!"

"My father," said Beatrice, feebly – and still, as she spoke, she kept her hand upon her heart – "wherefore didst thou inflict this miserable doom upon thy child?"

"Miserable!" exclaimed Rappaccini. "What mean you, foolish girl? Dost thou deem it misery to be endowed with marvellous gifts, against which no power nor strength could avail an enemy? Misery, to be able to quell the mightiest with a breath? Misery, to be as terrible as thou art beautiful? Wouldst thou, then, have preferred the condition of a weak woman, exposed to all evil, and capable of none?"

"I would fain have been loved, not feared," murmured Beatrice, sinking down upon the ground.– "But now it matters not; I am going, father, where the evil, which thou hast striven to mingle with my being, will pass away like a dream – like the fragrance of these poisonous flowers, which will no longer taint my breath among the flowers of Eden. Farewell, Giovanni! Thy words of hatred are like lead within my heart – but they, too, will fall away as I ascend. Oh, was there not, from the first, more poison in thy nature than in mine?"

To Beatrice – so radically had her earthly part been wrought upon by Rappaccini's skill – as poison had been life, so the powerful antidote was death. And thus the poor victim of man's ingenuity and of thwarted nature, and of the fatality that attends all such efforts of perverted wisdom, perished there, at the feet of her father and Giovanni. Just at that moment, Professor Pietro Baglioni looked forth from the window, and called loudly, in a tone of triumph mixed with horror, to the thunder-stricken man of science: "Rappaccini! Rappaccini! And is this the upshot of your experiment?"

FIRESTONE BOOKS' EARLY SCIENCE FICTION SERIES

We hope you enjoyed this book. You may be interested to know that Firestone Books also have a separate volume of early science fiction tales, available in paperback and as an eBook:

Early Science Fiction Tales 1: 51BC-1638AD

This first anthology, contains the earliest science fiction tales ever written, including:

The Dream of Scipio, True History, Icaro-Menippus, Urashima Taro, The Ebony Horse, The City of Brass, The Tale of the Bamboo Cutter and *The Man in the Moone.*

Firestone Books also has a number of early science fiction tales available as separate eBooks:

Book 1

The Dream of Scipio by Cicero – Written in 51BC, this tale tells of a man's dream of ascending into space.

Book 2

True History by Lucian of Samosata – Written around 160, this story tells of a man's ship being sucked up by a waterspout and being deposited on the Moon.

Book 3

Icaro-Menippus by Lucian of Samosata – In this tale, written around 160, a Grecian tells of his space journey, first to the Moon and then to the land of the gods.

Book 4

Urashima Taro – This traditional Japanese story, written around the eighth century, tells of a young man's journey three hundred years into the future.

Book 5

The Ebony Horse – This traditional Persian tale, written around 900, tells of a prince's adventures on a mechanical flying horse.

Book 6

The City of Brass – Written around the tenth century, this Persian story tells of a group of traveller's journey to a ghost town made of brass.

Book 7

The Tale of the Bamboo Cutter – This beautiful Japanese tale, written around 900, tells of a young girl's exile from the Moon and eventual return home with her fellow Moon People.

Book 8

The New Atlantis by Francis Bacon – This story tells of a man's discovery of an island populated by a culturally and scientifically advanced race of people.

Book 9

The Man in the Moone by Francis Godwin – This tale, first published in 1638, tells of a man's journey to the Moon where he discovers a Utopian world.

Book 10

Micromegas by Voltaire – This story first published in 1752, tells of two extraterrestrials visiting the Earth.

We hope to add more works to our growing collection, and for more information on the latest publications please visit:

www.firestonebooks.com

You can also find out more by following us on Facebook and Twitter

www.ingramcontent.com/pod-product-compliance
Lightning Source LLC
Chambersburg PA
CBHW071311250626
47159CB00004B/1389
* 9 7 8 1 9 0 9 6 0 8 0 8 5 *